40p

MURDER NOT
PROVEN?

To Maggie Allen
without whom . . . .

Jack House

MURDER NOT PROVEN?

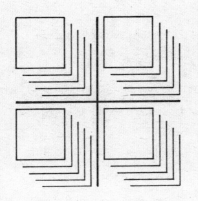

RICHARD DREW PUBLISHING

GLASGOW

First published 1984 by
Richard Drew Publishing Ltd.
6 Clairmont Gardens
Glasgow G3 7LW
Copyright © 1984 Jack House

Edited by Antony Kamm
Designed by James W. Murray

ISBN 0-86267-065-9

Typeset by John Swain & Son (Glasgow) Limited
in VIP Garamond
Printed and bound in Great Britain by Cox and Wyman Ltd.

The publisher is grateful to Tom Tullett,
Edinburgh City Libraries, and the Mitchell Library, Glasgow,
for help with illustrations.
He has made every effort to trace
the owners of copyright photographs,
and where he has failed to do so
he will be pleased to make the necessary arrangements
at the first opportunity.

Contents

Introduction

'N ot Proven" is a murder verdict known, as far as I am aware, only in Scotland. I have to be careful about this, but such is the Scottish influence throughout the world, that it may well be that some far-off country, seduced by the bagpipes, the kilt and – who knows? – usquebaugh, has followed Scotland's example. Scottish Law differs in other marked degrees from English Law, and especially in the matter of the conduct of a trial.

Most countries have only two verdicts, Guilty or Not Guilty. Scotland has the three, Guilty, Not Proven or Not Guilty. There have always been arguments about the Not Proven verdict which, according to some cynics, means "Go away and don't do it again!" I deal with the differing opinions at the end of this book.

The most famous of all "Not Proven" cases is that of the Glasgow belle of the ball, Madeleine Smith, who was charged with the murder by poison of her Channel Islander lover, Pierre Emile L'Angelier, at her home in Blythswood Square, Glasgow. Her trial was held in the High Court in Edinburgh because the authorities felt that the feeling in Glasgow was against her. The jury (by the way, a jury in Scotland numbers fifteen, unlike most juries elsewhere) found the case Not Proven, which annoyed Madeleine very much since she fully expected to hear the foreman say "Not Guilty". But I have dealt with her case at some length in my *Square Mile of Murder* and so I have not repeated it here, except for this honourable mention!

Of the four cases I have chosen, you will observe that the first was found "Guilty". But there was so much doubt about the guilt of John Watson Laurie that, when it was found that the jury's vote was eight for Guilty and seven for Not Proven, a large proportion of the public in Scotland called for his reprieve.

The second and fourth cases are straightforward "Not Proven" verdicts, and it is, to say the least, interesting to learn what followed in the fortunes of Alfred John Monson, the London con man, and John Donald Merrett, a student at Edinburgh University who had money troubles with his mother. The third case, the Portencross mystery, I have included because it was never solved, so that I am leaving it to the reader to draw his own conclusions and decide what his verdict would be.

One other thing interests me strongly. Three of these cases took place in one of the most beautiful estuaries in the world, the Firth of Clyde. In *Square Mile of Murder* I pointed out that four famous cases had their being in one square mile of the West End of Glasgow. And now we have three more cases in the Firth of Clyde. Is there something about the West of Scotland which encourages murder?

In that book too I demonstrated that the possible reason for the events was the Victorian idea of respectability. As you will see, that idea persists in *Murder Not Proven?* If other people think you are respectable, you may well get away with – well, murder.

Jack House
Glasgow,
October, 1983

THE GOATFELL CASE

John Watson Laurie

1

An Englishman meets a Scotsman

July 1889 was a wonderful month for holiday-makers. The seaside resorts, in particular, were packed with happy people. The sun shone all day and the evenings were balmy. Only the rich went abroad for the summer. For the vast majority of the population, England, Scotland, Wales and Ireland offered everything they wanted for a perfect summer.

July 1889 was also a wonderful month for murder. The general idea is that murder is a wintry affair. But most of our greatest murders have been committed during the summer holidays. In July 1889 the mathematically-minded murderer, Jack the Ripper, killed his seventh and last victim in Whitechapel. That was on the 18th of the month. On 31 July the trial began in Liverpool of Mrs. Maybrick, accused of killing her husband by the administration of arsenic. And on 15 July a young Englishman died on the top of a mountain in the Firth of Clyde. Later a young Scotsman was convicted of his murder.

The last of these murders, if it was a murder, took place on the Isle of Arran in the Firth of Clyde, still a popular holiday place but then, in 1889, far more than popular, especially during the Glasgow Fair Holidays. The island, in fact, was packed for the whole summer when, for the only time in the year, there were more people than deer within its sixty-mile circumference.

To many people Arran is an enchanted island. It is a geological freak, since it contains practically every rock formation in the whole of Britain. There are jagged mountains in the north, with some of the best climbing in Europe, and there are long beaches in the south, where palms grow in the open. Arran, in fact, is considered to be the epitome of Scotland, since every kind of Scottish scenery can be seen in this one place. There are other beautiful islands in the Firth of Clyde, which is really a miniature sea containing 1240 square miles of salt water. But, appropriately, Arran holds the palm.

Our story, however, starts on one of the other islands in the Firth, the Isle of Bute, which is smaller than Arran but has a bigger population. The capital of Bute is the town of Rothesay, and in Victorian days it was known as "the Madeira of the Clyde", and the wits of the day said it was so called because it took the cake! The young man on the deck of the Clyde steamer sailing across Rothesay Bay to the harbour may well have been one of those wits because he liked to cut a dash. It was Saturday, 6 July, and he was down from Glasgow on his holidays. He wore his "Sunday suit" and a straw hat, known locally as a "straw basher". He carried a bag and a coat and he had a card-case holding visiting cards which bore the name John Annandale and he would give his address as 6 Cambridge Street, Glasgow.

Now, John Annandale was not this young man's name, nor was 6 Cambridge Street his address. His real name was John Watson Laurie, and he lived in digs at 106 North Frederick Street, Glasgow. He was 26 years of age and worked as a pattern-maker in the Atlas Locomotive Engine Works in Springburn. He had fair hair and a fair moustache, and he could fairly talk. Some people didn't like him because he was conceited and always showing off. As things turned out,

Laurie's "false name" was to get him into very serious trouble indeed, but it was quite common to assume a new identity on holiday. Laurie was just following a common pattern for young men who did rather humdrum work at home and got all dressed up when they went on holiday.

They put on the dog in accent as well as dress, and they often gave a false name and address. I remember my father telling me that when you "clicked" with a young lady on holiday, especially at the beginning of the occasion, it was considered rather smart, if she asked for your address, to say "Number 77 Duke Street". This was the former number of the entrance to Duke Street Prison in Glasgow, though it was later blocked up when prisoners were taken in by the back door instead of the front. The young men were not doing this for criminal reasons. It was just that they thought their own names and addresses were not posh enough. And, as the young ladies they met were probably behaving in precisely the same way, there was no harm done.

This Annandale/Laurie chap, however, was rather a trial to his family. The Lauries were well-to-do people who lived in Coatbridge and this son showed signs of becoming the black sheep of the family. They had been considerably worried earlier that year when they were told by the Glasgow police that their son John was to appear in Glagow Sheriff Court on a charge of stealing jewellery from his landlady's house to the value of £18. John was convicted of this theft but, as the family had paid the £18 back to the landlady, he got off with an admonition.

Some people in Coatbridge thought that John Watson Laurie was "not all there". It was rumoured that there had been insanity in the Laurie family. But most people did not think Laurie was daft, though he was boastful and apt to embroider the truth. And, going back to the card with the false name, it was interesting to know that Laurie expected, indeed hoped, that in Rothesay he would meet people from the Coatbridge district who would know his real name and address.

The steamer slid in to Rothesay pier and those who had decided to holiday in Bute disembarked. Instead of making enquiries in Rothesay, Laurie went on to the contiguous village of Port Bannatyne, where the digs would be cheaper. In Iona Place he found a Mrs. Currie who had a room to let and handed over his nice, engraved "Annandale" card. Mrs. Currie thought he was a pleasant young chap and let the room to him.

For the next day or two Laurie spent more time in Rothesay than he did in Port Bannatyne. His object was to meet the Coatbridge girl whom he had courted and who had turned him down. She was a young girl teacher and she was on holiday in Rothesay with a male teacher friend. They did meet but Laurie felt that, if he were to get his wish and "cut out" the male teacher, he must be better dressed. And so, the following Tuesday, he took an early steamer back to the mainland and went to Glasgow by train. That night he reappeared at Mrs. Currie's in Port Bannatyne arrayed in a stylish brown knickerbocker suit and bright stockings – and, of course, the straw basher.

But this did not appear to touch the girl's heart either and Laurie told Mrs. Currie that he was going on a cruise to Inveraray on Loch Fyne. On the Glasgow Fair Friday he had second thoughts and decided to go to Arran. So that morning he went to Rothesay pier and joined the steamer *Ivanhoe,* which sailed through the entrancing Kyles of Bute to Corrie, Brodick, Lamlash and Whiting Bay on the Isle of Arran.

As the *Ivanhoe* left the pier and sailed towards the Kyles of Bute John Watson Laurie wandered around the steamer. A favourite cruise from Rothesay was the one to Arran and he thought his inamorata might be aboard. But she was nowhere to be seen, and he settled in a place on the main deck where he could look at the scenery and his fellow

Edwin Robert Rose

passengers at the same time. After the *Ivanhoe* had left Tighnabruaich he noticed a young man eyeing him from across the deck. This young man was a rather dashing looking chap – a "toff" in the vernacular of the time. He was slightly taller than Laurie, he wore a white yachting cap and a chocolate striped white blazer and white flannels, and he had a fine, dark flowing moustache.

But, though he looked a toff, this young man was cutting a

15

dash on his holidays too. He was Edwin Robert Rose, 32 years of age, and actually a clerk employed by a builder in Brixton. He was having his fortnight's holidays and had gone to the Glenburn Hydropathic in Rothesay because a friend of the family, the Rev. Gustavus Goodman, was staying there.

Edwin Robert Rose was a very affable young Englishman. He was full of high spirits, liked athletic pursuits and was ready to get into conversation with anybody. In those days he was one of a type known as "Cheerful Charlies". And now, on the deck of the *Ivanhoe,* he looked across at the fair young Scotsman. Then he made up his mind, walked over to Laurie and said, "Excuse me, haven't I met you in the Hydro?" With these simple words Edwin Robert Rose sealed his doom.

Laurie replied no, that they hadn't met in the Hydro, and Rose laughed and said, "It doesn't matter. We've met now, haven't we?" He introduced himself as Edwin Rose and Laurie gave him one of the engraved cards with the name John Annandale on it. Then, no doubt, they started talking of the splendid scenery. So this fatal friendship began.

As the *Ivanhoe* sailed from the Kyles into the Sound of Bute, the two young men saw the great Wagnerian background of the mountains of Arran. Then they sailed down to Corrie and there was Goatfell, with its eternal challenge to young, active men. Rose's friend Annandale said he'd climbed Goatfell several times, although there is no proof that he had ever been up the mountain in his life. Rose was captivated by the sight and the challenge and decided he must have a go at the mountain. Would Annandale be good enough to show him the way to the summit? Annandale agreed at once, and it was arranged that once they'd returned to Rothesay from the cruise, they would get together, plan a Fair weekend in Arran and climb Goatfell.

What was passing through the mind of John Watson Laurie as the *Ivanhoe* sailed into Brodick Bay we do not know. Had he, even then, formed some sort of plan to "deal" with his new found friend because, although Rose didn't know it, Laurie was already jealous of Rose's appearance and dashing, easy ways. Rose must have money, he thought. Or was he flattered that such an obvious toff should be acting in such an agreeable fashion towards him? Or did he merely think of making advance arrangements for staying in Brodick while they climbed Goatfell?

The *Ivanhoe* bumped Brodick pier and the two new friends stepped down the steep gangway and on to the Isle of Arran. Today there is a line of fair-sized hotels leading to the centre of the capital of Arran, but in 1889 there were few buildings in the area of the pier. If you wanted to get to the old Brodick, which lay round the bay under the shadow of Brodick Castle, you had to walk through the village of Invercloy, today's Brodick. When Laurie and Rose reached Invercloy, Laurie suggested that his friend should go out towards Brodick and they could meet again in Invercloy before catching the cruise steamer back to Rothesay. Meanwhile he would see about getting digs for their return to Arran. The enthusiastic Rose agreed at once, since he wanted to see as much of this marvellous island as possible. Off he walked towards Brodick.

Laurie knew it would be difficult to get any sort of holiday accommodation at all in Invercloy. He walked round the village, making enquiries without success. Then he went into Wooley's Tea Room, bought himself a cup of tea and asked if anyone there knew of digs to be had. A waitress said yes, just round the corner, ask for Mrs. Walker.

So Laurie walked down a lane beside the tea room, saw a name-plate with Walker on it, and soon Mrs. Walker was showing him the only accommodation she had left. There was not a vacant room in the house, but here was what is called in Glasgow a "single-end". It was an outhouse attached to the boarding house but there was no communication between them. The outhouse had its separate door. Laurie looked in and saw a rather dingy room with some odds and ends of furniture, including a rickety dressing-table with a wash-basin on it.

Mrs. Walker was quite surprised when this young man said that the room would be perfectly satisfactory. He explained that he'd like to take it for a week, and she said the charge would be seventeen shillings, including breakfast in her boarding house. Laurie handed her the card bearing the name of John Annandale and said that he had just come from Tighnabruaich. He said he'd be back the following day and, almost as an afterthought, mentioned that he would have a friend with him. Would it be possible for his friend to share the room? His friend would only be staying till the Wednesday. Mrs. Walker said the bed was big enough for two, and Mr. Annandale's friend could share the room for an extra charge of three shillings. But he'd have to take his meals outside. He could get breakfast every morning at Wooley's. Mr. Annandale indicated that everything in the garden was lovely.

It was now time to walk to Brodick pier to catch the *Ivanhoe* on her way back to Rothesay. Laurie met the enthusiastic Rose on the pier and the Englishman rhapsodised on the beauties of Arran. He was delighted when Laurie told him about the arrangements he had made for their stay. They agreed that they would meet next day and return to Brodick. As they sailed into Rothesay Rose pointed out the imposing Glenburn Hydropathic on its hill above the Bay and asked Laurie if he had ever been there. He was astonished when his new-found friend said no, and at once invited Laurie to come up to the Hydro for a drink that evening.

You can imagine the Springburn pattern-maker going back to his comparatively lowly digs in Port Bannatyne and thinking of his entry into the swanky world of the Glenburn Hydro in a few hours. When Laurie did turn up at the

Glenburn, Rose was having a drink with two friends of his who were also staying there. At once he introduced Mr. Annandale to Mr. Mickel and Mr. Thom, who came from Linlithgow. They weren't really friends, for Rose had just met them as casually as he had met Laurie. But Rose was a little friend of all the world.

He asked them to show Mr. Annandale round the delights of the Hydro while he changed out of his white yachting cap, his chocolate-striped blazer and his white flannels. John Watson Laurie must have thought to himself that he was really seeing high life at last.

They spent the rest of the evening talking and laughing and Rose was delighted with his new friend. Not so, Mickel and Thom. The Scots are notoriously critical of the Scots and the two canny chaps from Linlithgow were not enamoured of Annandale's put-on accent, or the way in which he either talked too much about himself and his prowess, or else seemed to relapse into the sulks and not talk at all.

Still, they all got on well enough to arrange that next morning the four of them would take the steamer to Brodick, although Mickel and Thom had not arranged accommodation there. Their plan was to spend the weekend in Arran and go back on the Monday, the day on which Rose and Laurie planned to climb Goatfell.

Late in the evening Rose saw his guest to the terrace outside the Hydro and wished him good luck on his way back to Port Bannatyne. As Laurie turned to go down the steps, Rose shouted after him "Annandale, I can't tell you how much I'm looking forward to Goatfell."

"So am I," said John Watson Laurie and walked a trifle unsteadily down the steps.

2

Death on the mountain

The morning after the night-out at the Glenburn Hydro John Watson Laurie walked from Port Bannatyne to Rothesay Pier and there met his three friends. Edwin Rose was delighted to see him. Mickel and Thom seemed to Laurie to be a trifle stand-offish, so that made him all the more talkative. They had another pleasant sail through the Kyles of Bute, across to the Isle of Arran, and duly disembarked at Brodick. Laurie and Rose walked into Invercloy with Mickel and Thom, who set off to find somewhere to stay for the weekend. They arranged to meet later that afternoon, and the two younger men went down the lane by Wooley's Tea Room to Mrs. Walker's house. Their landlady greeted them, showed them to the hut and left a key with Laurie.

Meanwhile the two Linlithgow men were tramping around Invercloy and even farther afield in their search for rooms. There wasn't even a spare bed in the village – it appeared that Laurie and Rose had got the last one. Mickel and Thom were so dispirited that they decided to take the evening steamer back to Rothesay, but just then they met a friend who had a yacht anchored in Brodick Bay. He invited them to spend the weekend aboard his boat and they were delighted to agree.

When they met Rose and Laurie they told their story and Rose was delighted that they had found accommodation aboard the yacht. Laurie seemed in one of his sulky moods, but brightened up when they went for drinks to one of the Invercloy hotels. So they spent Fair Saturday but hardly met again over the weekend because on the Sunday the Linlithgow men walked over the hill road south to Lamlash. Laurie and Rose walked through the beautiful Glen Rosa to the north and considered walking on to the village of Corrie, but felt it was going to take too long.

Later that evening they met Mickel and Thom who bore an invitation to them to row out to a party aboard their friend's yacht. Rose jumped at the chance but Laurie said he was afraid an attack of toothache was coming on, and he went back to the single-end while Rose set sail for the yacht. Well, we know from the works of Robert Burns that toothache is "the hell o' a' diseases", so that could possibly explain what happened later that Sabbath night. An old Arran woman who lived in the cluster of cottages behind Wooley's Tea Room saw the fair young man from Tighnabruaich (everybody in Invercloy knew everybody else's business) walking up and down the lane beside Mrs. Walker's house, talking to himself and looking very odd. "The Deil's busy wi' that young chap", was her verdict. But, if Laurie was suffering from toothache, what could be more appropriate than the spiritual presence of the Devil beside a sufferer from the hell o' a' diseases?

On Fair Monday morning Mickel was having a stroll through Invercloy. His aim was to get some extra provisions for the yacht, so he went into Wooley's shop. There, at the tea room, he saw Rose having his customary lonely breakfast. He went over to pass the time of day, and Rose told him that he was going to climb Goatfell with John Annandale that afternoon. Mickel's doubts about Annandale came to the surface. He pointed out to Rose that, although Annandale talked so much at times, he had never indicated where he came from or what he did. He counselled Rose to get rid of Annandale and warned him not to climb the mountain with the strange young man.

Edwin Rose agreed right away that he would not go up Goatfell with John Annandale. Mickel explained that he and Thom were returning to Rothesay by the 3.30 steamer, and Rose immediately said that he'd be at the pier to see his friends off. It is the time-honoured custom in Brodick for people to see their friends off from the pier. Mickel, looking down from the deck at the crowd, saw that Rose was there all right, waving cheerily and shouting his goodbyes. But he had Annandale with him. Not only that, but Rose had discarded his yachting cap, blazer and flannels, and was now dressed for climbing, complete with heavy boots, leggings and a waterproof.

The steamer swept its graceful way out of Brodick Bay and that was the last that Mr. Mickel and Mr. Thom ever saw of their pleasant young friend from London. Rose kept waving until the steamer was well out in the bay. Then he and John Watson walked off the pier and trudged through Invercloy and Brodick on to the lower slopes of Goatfell.

Arran is second only to the Isle of Skye in providing difficult peaks for climbers in Scotland. But Goatfell, though the highest point of the island, is not one of them. First there is a steady pull up the hillside and then a ridge which leads to the last two hundred feet, which becomes a rock scramble which is not difficult for any active person. I have followed in the steps of Laurie and Rose and, though I suffer from vertigo, I have been to the summit of Goatfell. I must admit, though, that I didn't linger long on the top, because the scenery was too awe-inspiring for me. Looking to the west and to the north I saw jagged peaks and ragged ridges and terrifying descents, just short of sheer precipices. It was a magnificent scene, but my knees were shaking. I have been on much higher mountains in Europe but have not felt the elemental danger which seemed to surround me on Goatfell. Perhaps I was thinking too much of Laurie and Rose.

They walked up through the grounds of Brodick Castle to reach the open moorland. As they climbed, they met two men coming down. Laurie recognised them at once. They were relatives of Mrs. Walker and had breakfast with Laurie every morning. Naturally, they had seen Rose about the place as well. They thought it was rather late for people to begin climbing Goatfell, but holiday-makers are queer folk and there's no saying what strange ideas they'll get next. They just said hello and walked on.

Well up the hillside the two young men, with Laurie always leading the way, overtook a party of three climbers. They were the Rev. Robert Hind of Paisley, with his friends, the Rev. Joseph Ritson and John McCabe. Laurie walked past the ministerial party with never a word and continued climbing. Edwin Rose, however, couldn't pass anyone without chatting. In conversation he told them that he was from London, but was staying in Rothesay for a holiday and that the young man in front was his guide.

A thunder shower came on and the Rev. Robert Hind's party prudently took shelter behind some boulders. The two young men put on their waterproofs and kept on climbing and, as they came to that last rock scramble, they passed a man resting on a boulder. His name was Edward Francis and he came from London. His brother Fred was already on the top of Goatfell, and Edward now fell in behind Laurie and Rose and completed the climb with them.

When they were all on the summit of the mountain, the Francis brothers had some conversation with Rose. But Laurie said not a word. He stood off on his own and contemplated the peaks and the ridges and the terrifying gullies. Edwin Rose asked the Francis brothers about the various ways down from the top of Goatfell. It seemed that he did not want to return by the normal, well-worn route. But the Francis brothers were new to Arran and had no advice to give. It was about six o'clock in the evening and just then the Rev. Robert Hind led his party over the rocks to the summit. They wanted to catch the 8.30 steamer at Brodick so they had not much time to spare for the view. But they did see the young Englishman and the young Scotsman standing towards the farther end of the summit, looking in the direction of Glen Sannox. Then they left the young men on the top and started downhill again. Occasionally they looked behind them as they descended, but saw no sign of the couple and decided that they must have taken the track down by the Saddle between Glen Rosa and Glen Sannox.

Meanwhile the Francis brothers, who were keen photographers, spent twenty minutes or so taking every view which caught their fancy. Then they packed up and at 6.25 left the summit and climbed down the steep track. As they went they saw the two young men standing on a boulder with their backs to Ailsa Craig and pointing to the north. The brothers assumed they were discussing the direction of their descent. And that was the last time that anyone, other than John Watson Laurie, alias Annandale, saw Edwin Robert Rose alive.

Some three hours later, however, a young Arran shepherd did see John Watson Laurie. The shepherd, David McKenzie from High Corrie, was employing the long, light July night in "daffing" with a couple of maids employed in Sannox boarding houses. The three of them were leaning against the wall of the old Sannox graveyard in a leafy lane. McKenzie saw a tired-looking man come down Glen Sannox and cut through a field beside the graveyard in the direction of Corrie. He mentioned the man to his girlfriends, but they paid no attention.

The worn-out figure which staggered down the Glen was John Watson Laurie. Apparently his task of guiding Edwin Rose to the top of Goatfell was over.

Just about ten o'clock that night a Greenock law clerk,

James Wilson, was standing at the hole-in-the-wa' bar in Corrie Hotel, having a quiet drink. A stranger suddenly appeared and asked Wilson to order a bottle of beer for him, as "time" had gone. But they weren't too strict in the Corrie Hotel in Victorian days and Wilson told the stranger that he'd get the beer all right if he ordered it himself. The stranger was John Watson Laurie. He drank his beer and then asked for a gill bottle to be filled with whisky, as he was going to walk the six miles to Brodick.

Again Laurie disappeared from human ken. No one saw him on his way back to Brodick. His landlady in Invercloy, Mrs. Walker, paid no attention to the outhouse and didn't know whether her boarders had come in or not.

The first steamer for Ardrossan, the nearest mainland port, left Brodick at seven o'clock every morning, except Sundays of course. On that Tuesday of the Glasgow Fair a young medical student from Linlithgow went to catch the *Scotia* and whom should he meet but the "John Annandale" he had been introduced to by his friends Mickel and Thom, who also came from Linlithgow. Naturally, the medical student talked to Annandale and travelled as far as Greenock with him. He even helped Annandale with his luggage.

Probably the young student had not had the opportunity of seeing the luggage which Rose and Annandale brought with them from Rothesay to Brodick. When they disembarked at Brodick Pier, Rose had a smart black leather bag, while Annandale had a rather shabby brown one. Now in the train for Glasgow Annandale had two bags, one brown and one in black leather.

Just about the time that Annandale arrived in Glasgow and became John Watson Laurie once more, Mrs. Walker in Brodick was wondering why he hadn't come into breakfast as usual. But she knew that he and Rose had planned to climb Goatfell the day before and decided they were having a "long lie".

Still, when it got to 11 a.m., she thought it was time they were getting up, and went to the outhouse to wake them. She knocked on the door, but there was no answer. She opened the door and found the room empty, though the bed looked as if it had been slept in. In a corner there were a tennis racket, a pair of slippers, an old waterproof, and a straw basher.

Mrs. Walker was a woman of experience, particularly as regards holidaymakers at the Glasgow Fair. She realised that she'd been done by this young man, Annandale, who had promised to pay £1 for his and his friend's lodgings for the week. She realised too that her boarders must have left by the early morning boat and there was nothing she could do about it, except to write to John Annandale.

Well, there was one other thing she could do about it, and that was report the incident to the police. But she thought that wasn't worth bothering about. She had lost £1 and that was that. She did tell some of her friends, of course, and, as was inevitable in Invercloy, the police got to hear about it. This was the busiest time of the year for the Arran police and they decided the theft of £1 was not a major crime. They were to be proved wrong.

That very Tuesday afternoon who should arrive back at Mrs. Currie's in Iona Place, Port Bannatyne, but her lodger, the pleasant John Annandale? And this time he had changed his clothes and was wearing a white yachting cap, a chocolate striped blazer and white flannels – a real toff, and no mistake. He told Mrs. Currie that he had had a pleasant time in Arran and had climbed Goatfell. In his dashing new clothes he sought out the female teacher, but, once again, he pressed his suit in vain. He spent a lot of time in Rothesay but the one place he did not visit was the Glenburn Hydropathic.

At the Hydro only one of Edwin Rose's friends was left – the Rev. Gustavus Goodman. He had received a letter from Rose on Tuesday, 16 July, dated from "Mrs. Walker's, Brodick", and saying he would be back on Wednesday to collect his letters and say goodbye. When Edwin didn't turn up on the Wednesday, Mr. Goodman assumed that he'd gone straight to London from Arran instead of stopping off at Rothesay. He had already paid his bill at the Hydro and had all his belongings with him so, apart from collecting letters and saying goodbye, there was no special reason why he should return to Rothesay.

Over on the Isle of Arran the young Englishman was by this time forgotten, except perhaps by Mrs. Walker of Invercloy. Certainly Mr. Davidson, the farmer in Glen Rosa, did not know of Rose's existence. In those days the last house as you went up Glen Rosa from the String Road leading across the island from Brodick belonged to the Davidson family, who had lived in Arran for many years. Mr. Davidson kept his sheep over as much of Goatfell as sheep were able to go and, during the Glasgow Fair Week of 1889, he was up on the mountainside with his two dogs, making sure his sheep were safe.

As the farmer was crossing a ridge above a steep gully, his dogs dashed down the mountain side and started circling round a big boulder, barking furiously. He thought they were after a rabbit and whistled them back. He never thought for a moment of investigating the boulder. Why should he? But if he had been more curious, or if he had just decided to go down that way with his dogs, what had happened to Edwin Robert Rose might have been discovered two weeks earlier than it was.

Edwin Rose was due to arrive in London on Thursday, 18 July, and his brother Benjamin went to the station to meet him. When Edwin did not arrive, Benjamin was rather perturbed. Although Edwin was inclined to be a dashing character when on holiday, he was a very conscientious young man in Balham. The Rose family held a conclave and decided to send a wire to the Rev. Goodman, who was, incidentally, a brother of the Brixton builder for whom Edwin Rose worked as a clerk.

The very day they sent their wire, John Annandale was swanking it around Rothesay in a white yachting cap, a chocolate striped blazer and white flannels. But he suddenly became John Watson Laurie again when he met a friend of his from Glasgow.

This friend was James G. Aitken, a grain salesman from Shawlands, and the first thing that struck Mr. Aitken was that the white yachting cap which Laurie was wearing was remarkably like the cap that he'd seen a young Englishman wearing aboard the *Ivanhoe* on Fair Friday. That was the last time Aitken had met Laurie, and Laurie had pointed out this Englishman, said his name was Rose, and that he was going to spend a few days with him in Arran.

However, Aitken said nothing about the yachting cap, and all Laurie said in reply to his query about how they'd got on in Brodick was, "Oh, very well." Laurie added that his holiday was over and he was going back to Glasgow.

That night Laurie asked Mrs. Currie, his landlady at Port Bannatyne, to let him have his breakfast the following morning at 8.30, as he was going to see a friend off on the nine o'clock steamer. On the Saturday morning his fortnight's holiday was up and he asked Mrs. Currie to have his bill and his lunch ready for him at 1 p.m. He was going for a stroll after he'd seen his friend off.

He went out after breakfast and didn't come back. Mrs. Currie had a bill for £3 3s 8d on her hands. She did send it to John Annandale, 6 Cambridge Street, Glasgow, but was told there was no such person there. She searched her lodger's room, but found only a white yachting cap and a pair of tennis shoes – which she thought odd because Mr. Annandale didn't play tennis.

Since his holiday was ending it was almost time for John Watson Laurie to give up his pose as John Annandale. But he had one last shot as he left Rothesay that Saturday aboard the steamer *Caledonia*. Just as she was turning in Rothesay Bay she ran down a small boat. The *Caledonia* purser asked for witnesses and one passenger immediately stepped forward, volunteered to be a witness, and handed over his card. It bore the name Annandale but a few days later when a clerk from the Caledonian Railway Company went to see Mr. Annandale at the North Frederick Street address on the card, he found that no such person was known there.

And now we go back to Rothesay and the Rev. Gustavus Goodman who, like so many holidaymakers on the Clyde, had been moving around the Firth so much that he didn't get Benjamin Rose's telegram until Monday, 22 July. Mr. Goodman left the Glenburn Hydro at once and took the first boat to Brodick. He soon found Mrs. Walker, who told her story of the two young lodgers, how they left to climb Goatfell on Fair Monday and how the following day she'd discovered their luggage was gone and she had seen neither of them since. Her bill had not been paid either. Mr. Goodman went straight to the Brodick Police Station and told his story.

On Saturday, 27 July, Benjamin Rose arrived in Brodick from London. He and the police wanted to know what had happened to his brother Edwin. They were in the wrong place from the point of view of getting information. If they had only been in Rothesay that afternoon they might have met the missing John Annandale. Who should again meet John Watson Laurie there but his old friend, James Aitken, the Shawlands grain merchant? Laurie said he was just down for the day. Doubtless he didn't bother going as far as Iona Place, Port Bannatyne, and eschewed a visit to Glenburn Hydro.

In Arran word soon went round Brodick and Corrie that a young Englishman was missing and that he had been last seen on the top of Goatfell. On Sunday, 28 July, a search party was formed. Natives of Arran and visitors to the island joined the party, but the weather was wet and misty and up on those dangerous hills visibility was sometimes under six feet. They had to give up the search. Small search parties were arranged for the following week and, if these were unsuccessful, the whole mountainside would be combed on the following Sunday, 4 August.

All this activity on the island came to the notice of the newspapers. The first headings, in a Glasgow paper on 29 July, were –

AN ARRAN MYSTERY
SUSPICIOUS DISAPPEARANCE OF AN
ENGLISH TOURIST
AN ACCIDENT OR A CRIME?

"What has become of the young man Rose is shrouded in mystery," said the newspaper. "He has not returned to his friends in England, and there is a growing suspicion that he never left the island."

The search parties were out in rain and mist all that week but found nothing. Then early on the morning of Sunday, 4 August, the rain stopped, the sun came out, the mists rolled away and the whole face of the majestic mountain was clear.

The searchers numbered two hundred – one hundred and fifty from Brodick and fifty from Corrie. The Brodick party gathered at Brodick Castle Kennels at 9 a.m. and split into three groups. The Corrie party was to go up by Glen Sannox, so the Brodick groups tackled the face. Sergeant Munro from the Lamlash police and the Brodick Castle gamekeeper led one group by the eastern ridge. Constable Munro of Brodick took his group straight up and Constable McColl of Shiskine climbed with his men by Glen Rosa. So from north, south, east and west the two hundred men slowly converged on the summit of Goatfell.

They were hampered by a sudden heavy mist which held up some of them for two hours. But eventually the second

The boulder.
The stick is placed where Rose's head was lying.

group from Brodick met the Corrie boys on the summit. There they divided again and some went down into Glen Rosa while others descended the ridge which runs from Goatfell to the Saddle. About half-way to the Saddle a Corrie fisherman named Francis Logan suddenly hallooed wildly. The search was over.

Francis Logan had noticed a strange smell on the mountainside and traced it to a large boulder in the Coire-na-Fuaren* – the very same boulder round which Farmer Davidson's collies had barked nearly two weeks ago. There was a cavity under the granite boulder and the opening had been elaborately built up with stones, turf and heather.

Everyone waited until Sergeant Munro arrived. He pulled away the barricade and there, lying face downwards beneath the boulder, was the body of Edwin Robert Rose. His head and face were terribly smashed. His pockets were empty. His tweed cap, folded in four, was found under a heavy stone in the bed of a nearby burn.

*Throughout the trial of Laurie this gully was described as the Corr-na-Fourin. On modern maps the name is printed as Coire-na-Fuaran – the Corrie (or Gully) of Springs.

3

The Annandale hunt

A goodly number of the searchers round the body of Edwin Robert Rose in the Coire-na-Fuaren had one thought in mind. Where was the mysterious John Annandale, who had gone up Goatfell with the murdered man? That ascent had been accomplished many days before the body was discovered so that, if John Annandale were alive, he had had plenty of time either to tell someone of his missing companion, or (if he had some kind of conscience about the occurrence) to get far, far away from the Isle of Arran. All that was known of John Annandale was his appearance and the fact that he came from Glasgow.

But in Glasgow John Watson Laurie's friend, James G. Aitken, had his suspicions. When he read in his newspaper on 29 July that an English holiday-maker named Rose was missing in Arran, he recollected that Laurie had pointed out Rose to him on the steamer to Brodick and said he was going to spend some time with his new friend in Arran. Then, Aitken recalled to himself, he had met Laurie in Rothesay a week later and had been struck by the fact that Laurie was wearing a white yachting cap which was remarkably like Rose's.

As a grain merchant, Aitken was a frequent visitor to the old Corn Exchange in Hope Street, Glasgow. He was standing outside the Exhange when he saw John Watson Laurie coming down the street. Aitken hailed Laurie and asked him immediately, "What do you know about this Arran mystery?"

Laurie, according to Aitken, "hummed and hawed" and Aitken said, "Dear me, have you not been reading the papers? Wasn't Rose the name of the party you intended going to Brodick with?" Laurie hesitated for a moment, then said, "It's the same name, but it can't be the same man. The Rose I was with came back to Glasgow with me and went on to Leeds."

"You should go to the police and tell them about Rose," counselled Aitken, and then he said suddenly, "Whose cap were you wearing that Friday when I met you in Rothesay?"

Laurie took a step back and gasped, "Surely you don't think I am a . . .?" He stopped there, but Aitken's impression was that he was going to add the word "thief". Then Laurie said he must speak to a passing friend and made to move. Aitken detained him long enough to make him agree to a meeting between them that night to have another talk about the Arran affair.

Laurie dashed off – but in the opposite direction from the passing friend! And when Aitken went to the appointed rendezvous that night, Laurie did not turn up. Aitken went straight to the Glasgow Central Police Station and said he thought that John Watson Laurie and John Annandale were one and the same man.

Naturally, the police wanted to interview John Watson Laurie. He could at least tell them where and when he had last seen Edwin Rose, whose body had not yet been found but whose disappearance was regarded as mysterious. But the bird had flown. When the police made enquiries at the Atlas Engineering Works in Springburn, where Laurie was a pattern-maker, they found that he had applied to his foreman for his wages that morning.

He explained to the foreman – and this is interesting in view of his conversation with the Shawlands grain merchant that morning – that he was leaving to become a traveller in the grain trade. But to one of his pals in the pattern-making shop Laurie said he was going to Leith on an engineering job. He added that he had a return railway ticket to London and that he'd been spending his holiday with a friend whom, he said, "I left in Arran."

That afternoon Laurie went to a pawnbroker's shop in Commercial Road and sold his pattern-maker's tools for twenty-five shillings. By the time he was due to meet his friend Aitken to discuss the Arran mystery he had already shaken the dust of the city from his feet.

The police went to see Laurie's father and mother at Coatbridge, but they knew nothing of the black sheep of the family. By this time the police were in no doubt that Laurie was "John Annandale".

On the day before the discovery of Edwin Rose's body on Goatfell, Mrs. King of North Frederick Street, Glasgow, took a letter to the police. It was from her erstwhile boarder, John Laurie. It was written in pencil and dated from Hamilton, near Glasgow, on 2 August.

"Dear Madam," wrote Laurie, "I beg to enclose P.O. for my rent, as I can't call, for I have to go to Leith. There are some people trying to get me into trouble, and I think you should give them no information at all, and I will prove to them how they are mistaken before very long.
                          Yours respectfully . . ."

Mrs. King was luckier than Mrs. Walker at Brodick or Mrs. Currie at Port Bannatyne because Laurie had never paid *them* any money for board and lodgings at all.

And so, although the men who found Rose's body below that boulder on the precipitous slope of the Coire-na-Fuaren did not know the identity of the Englishman's companion, the police in Glasgow did.

Eight of the two hundred searchers on Goatfell volunteered to carry the body the nine rough miles into Corrie. Down through the trackless reaches of Glen Sannox they went, down to the very burying-ground where the High Corrie shepherd had seen Laurie pass, and where Rose lies buried today. Down into the darkness of that August night, till they reached the Corrie Hotel at 1 a.m. and laid the body in the adjoining coach-house.

The Procurator Fiscal for Bute had already been told of the discovery of Rose's body and he had arranged for Dr. Fullarton of Lamlash and a Dr. Gilmour of Linlithgow who was on holiday in Arran at the time to be ready at the coach-house for the post-mortem. In the light of oil lamps, and with villagers from Corrie gathered round the open door of the coach-house, the post-mortem was carried out. The doctors' conclusion was that the injuries to Rose's head had been inflicted by repeated blows from some heavy instrument, probably a stone.

Reporting this the North British Daily Mail, published in Glasgow, said: "On the other hand it is thought a cowardly push from the murderer sent Rose reeling over the precipice, and that death not ensuing immediately, Annandale clambered after his helpless victim, and silenced for ever his futile cries for help. Be the method what it may, the whole circumstances point to murder in its blackest aspect, and murder by someone moved by feelings of more than fiendish malignity."

Newspapers, of course, were less inhibited in the Good Old Days than they are now. They made no secret of their opinion that Annandale should be caught and accused of the murder of Rose. Then, when it was revealed that Annandale was really John Watson Laurie, they turned their attack on him and on the police.

Four days after the body of Rose had been discovered the North British Daily Mail said in a leader: "We had hoped by this time Laurie would have been in their [the police's] hands. Short of going about the streets shouting 'I am John Annandale', Laurie did pretty nearly all that was possible to put the police on his track. What strikes one most strongly about his conduct since the night of the tragedy is his sheer stupidity.

"He acted with the utmost recklessness, apparently on the extraordinary assumption that no inquiry would be made regarding the missing gentleman by his relatives, or at least that the murder would remain unknown and that the body would never be discovered."

But the police, as sometimes happens, knew a little more than the newspapers or the public thought they knew. The favourite theory in the Coatbridge district was that John Watson Laurie had committed suicide. There was the greatest possible sympathy for his respected family. There were also rumours that Laurie had been seen in almost every town in the West of Scotland.

A workman found some food on the top of a wall round an old pit shaft at Mossend. Beside the food was a piece of paper with the words, "I'm the murderer!" written on it. The theory was that Laurie, overtaken by remorse, couldn't even eat his lunch and had cast himself into the pit. "But after a great deal of trouble on the part of the police," says William Roughead, the criminologist, "it was found that the pit, like the story, had nothing in it."

The hue and cry for John Watson Laurie was on. Everybody knew now that he was the John Annandale who had climbed Goatfell with Edwin Rose, whose mangled body was found hidden under a granite boulder on the side of Goatfell. The most outspoken newspaper was still the North British Daily Mail. They stung the police and they must have stung Laurie too, for he took the astounding step of writing a Letter to the Editor.

On Monday, 12 August, the North British Daily Mail

published a letter from Laurie, who had disappeared from Glasgow on 31 July. The letter bore a Liverpool postmark and it was handed to the Glasgow police who went into action at once. It was the first hard clue they'd had as to Laurie's whereabouts. The police didn't mind the letter being published, but they did advise the Editor to leave out the names which Laurie mentioned.

And this was Laurie's letter –

10th Aug., '89

Dear Editor,

I feel that I should write a long detailed letter to your paper, but I am in no mood to do so.

I rather smile when I read that my arrest is hourly expected. If things go as I have designed them, I will soon have arrived at the country from whose bourne no traveller returns, and since there has been so much said about me, it is only right that the public should know what are the real circumstances which has brought me to this.

Three years ago I became very much attached to Miss ——, teacher, —— School, and residing at ——. My affection for this girl was at first returned ... until I discovered that she was encouraging the attentions of another man, ——, teacher, ——, who took every opportunity to depreciate me in her estimation.

Since then I have been perfectly careless in what I did, and my one thought was how to punish her enough for the cruel wrong she had done me; and it was to watch her audacious behaviour that I went to Rothesay this and last year. I may say that I became acquainted with another young lady, whose good qualities I sincerely wish that I had learned to appreciate sooner, as if I had I would have been in a very different position today.

As regards Mr. Rose, poor fellow, no one who knows me will believe for one moment that I had any complicity in his death.

invited him.   12/8/89

We went to the top of
Goatfell where I left him
in the company of two men
who came from to Loch Ranza
and were going to Brodick

I went down to Corrie
and met some friends and
we afterwards visited went to the
Hotel where we met several
of the gentlemen who were
camping out and I left
for Brodick about ten

I could easily prove that
what I say is true, but
I decline to bring the
names of my friends
into this disgraceful affair
so will content myself

Part of Laurie's letter to the North British Daily Mail

The morning I left for Arran I was in the company of two friends on Rothesay pier when Mr. Rose came to me and said that he was going to spend a few days with me at Arran.

I was very much surprised at this, as my friends could vouch, for I had not invited him. We went to the top of Goatfell, where I left him in the company of two men who came from Loch Ranza, and were going to Brodick.

I went down to Corrie and met some friends, and we afterwards visited the hotel, where we met several of the gentlemen who were camping out, and I left for Brodick about 10.

I could easily prove that what I say is true, but I decline to bring the names of my friends into this disgraceful affair, so will content myself by wishing them a last adieu.

Yours truly,
John W. Laurie.

Presumably it was the young lady whose qualities Laurie wished he had appreciated sooner that he had met in Glasgow a week before he wrote this letter and took to Tillietudlem for a Saturday afternoon out. He saw her to her home in Coatbridge and spoke moodily and mysteriously of having to leave Glasgow. He said that it was the last time he would ever see her. She asked for an explanation, but Laurie refused to say any more.

Despite this dramatic farewell, Laurie 'phoned the girl early on the following Monday morning and made an appointment to meet her in Glasgow. She kept the appointment but Laurie did not turn up, for the very good reason that that was the very day he fled the city.

The Glasgow police were not interested in Laurie's new love affair, but they were interested in getting hold of Laurie. With modern methods of scientific investigation, with radio and television, with finger-printing and all the rest of the advantages the police enjoy today, they might have got Laurie sooner than they did. As it was, they went to Liverpool at once. They traced Laurie all right, but once again the bird had flown.

Laurie had arrived in Liverpool two days after Rose's body was found under the boulder at Goatfell. He got lodgings with a Mrs. Ennitt in 10 Greek Street, Liverpool and paid a week's rent in advance. (He seemed to have stopped bilking landladies by this time.) On Thursday, 8 August, however, a Liverpool newspaper published a story about the Arran mystery and identified "John Annandale" as John Watson Laurie.

That day Laurie told Mrs. Ennitt that he'd got a job in Manchester as a traveller in the cotton trade and must go there right away. He went in such a hurry that he left behind him a box containing some white shirts. When the police arrived Mrs. Ennitt showed them the box and the shirts. Each shirt had been stamped with the name "John W. Laurie".

These shirts were soon identified as having belonged to Edwin Rose. He had taken them with him to Rothesay when he went on holiday. But now Laurie had stamped his name on them.

The trail led to Manchester but the police found no Laurie there. All the time they were receiving reports from various parts of Britain that a man looking like Laurie had been seen. And then, on 27 August, the wanted man sent a second Letter to the Editor. This time it bore the Aberdeen postmark!

Having had one letter already published, Laurie may have fancied his literary style. At any rate, the second letter was sent to the Glasgow Herald, a somewhat superior newspaper to the North British Daily Mail.

"Sir," Laurie wrote, "I expected that the letter which I so foolishly addressed to the Mail would have been my last, but I read so many absurd and mad things in the daily papers that I feel it my duty to correct some of them. And the first of these is the assertion that I am kept out of the way by friends. I have not come across a friend since I left Glasgow, nor have I been in communication with any one. I don't deny the fact that I would like to meet some of my friends again, but I am more careful than allow myself to be lured like the moth to the flame. Although I am entirely guiltless of the crime I am so much wanted for, yet I can recognise that I am a ruined man in any case, so it is far from my intention to give myself up. I first went to Glasgow in the spring of 1882, but being among strangers I became homesick, so was glad of the offer held out to me of something to do at Uddingston. Messrs John Gray & Co. were at that time making a winding engine, also several steam cranes, for the underground railway, and during the months of June, July and August I assisted Mr. John Swan to make the patterns. I remember Mr. Swan as being a very nice gentleman, but I have no recollection of a man the name of Alexander. I was not at Hamilton eight weeks ago, and I certainly did not smile to Alexander on the way there. If I had travelled in a train where I was known, don't you think it likely that I would have left at the first stoppage? The stories about me being seen are all imagination. I have not been seen by any one who knows me, and I have been travelling all the time in England and Ireland, and as I can see that this is no land for me I will be off again. It is true that I did take a room for a week at 10 Greek Street, Liverpool, which I paid in advance. I only stayed three days. I did not board with the lady of the house, and after destroying my papers I left my box, with no intention of ever calling for it again, as it was an encumbrance to me. The Mail takes credit to itself in this case, which does not belong to it at all, for it was a friend of mine who felt it his duty to inform the authorities that Mr. Rose left Rothesay with me, and when I saw from an evening paper that Mr. Rose had not returned to his lodgings, I began at once to arrange for my departure, for I had told so many about him. Seemingly there was a motive to do away with poor Rose; it was not to secure his valuables. Mr. Rose was to all appearances worse off than myself, indeed he assured me that he had spent so much on his tour, that he had barely sufficient to last till he got home. He wore an old Geneva watch with no gold albert attached, and I am sure no one saw him wear a ring on his tour, and no one saw me wear one, and well [name deleted] knew that he was speaking a lie when he said that he saw me wear a ring at Rothesay. A nice picture this fellow made of me, purely out of ill-will, because I had fooled his precious brother. He says that when he saw me I was wearing a ring and had one of my hands gloved; this is a preposterous falsehood; indeed, his whole story from beginning to end was a lie. I met him one morning in Shamrock Street, not Cambridge Street, and I caught hold of his arm when he asked a boy to call a policeman, there was no striking on either side, but if there had been I leave those who know us to judge who would come off second best. However, these are trivial matters uninteresting to all but those immediately concerned, and as I am not inclined to say any more I hope this will be the last the public will hear of me.

Yours truly, John W. Laurie."

Although this ineffable letter was posted in Aberdeen, the Glasgow police believed that it was a blind on Laurie's part. They were certain that he was not far from his family's home at Coatbridge. His family could not stand all the dreadful publicity and had gone into purdah, refusing to communicate with friends or newspaper reporters.

On the afternoon of 3 September the stationmaster at Ferniegair, which was not far from the Tillietudlem Station to which Laurie had brought his second inamorata, was out on the platform waiting for the Glasgow train to arrive. He saw a man hanging about the station entrance and sent a boy to tell the man that, if he wanted the Glasgow train, he'd better hurry up. The boy did so, but the man muttered that he didn't want any train and walked quickly away.

Just then the local constable, James Gordon, who was going to spend his day off in Glasgow, arrived on the platform and the stationmaster told him he'd seen a man who looked like Laurie. The policeman went up on to the bridge over the line and saw a man hastening along the Carlisle road. He decided that this was more important than going to Glasgow and hurried after the stranger. When the man discovered that he was being followed, he suddenly bolted into a field, ran across the railway line and along the Lanark road.

Gordon gave chase, shouting, "Catch that man! That's Laurie!" Some Larkhall miners at a pit-head near by heard the shouts. They downed tools and took up the chase which led to the appropriately named Quarry Wood, a mile and a half from the station. This wood led down to the River Clyde and Gordon got the miners to surround it before he went in to look for Laurie.

Two small boys came out of the wood and said they'd seen a man hiding under bushes in the old quarry. So the hunters went into the wood and under a bush lay John Watson Laurie with a razor in his hand and his throat cut. But it was only a superficial wound and Laurie gasped out, "I'm Laurie, but not Rose's murderer. I wish I'd got time to do the job right. I was going to commit suicide tonight."

Constable Gordon cautioned him that anything he said might be used in evidence against him, and Laurie replied, "I robbed the man, but I didn't murder him."

4

Did he fall or was he pushed?

The trial of John Watson Laurie for the murder of Edwin Rose began in the High Court of Edinburgh on Friday, 8 November 1889. There were certain peculiarities about it. First of all, the customary day for starting an important murder trial in the Scottish Courts is Monday, giving the possibility of at least an open week for the hearing of the case. But the judge, Lord Kingsburgh, the Lord Justice-Clerk, intimated at the opening that this trial, started on a Friday, should be finished by Saturday. He did not have to give any reason for this decision, but it could have been that he did not like murder trials and hated having to don the Black Cap.

Second, it seemed odd to some people concerned with the case that the indictment read, "John Watson Laurie, prisoner in the prison of Greenock, you are indicted at the instance of the Right Honourable James Patrick Bannerman Robertson, Her Majesty's Advocate, and the charge against you is, that on 15th July, 1889, at Corr-na-Fourin, near the head of Glen Sannox, in the island of Arran, Buteshire, you did assault Edwin Robert Rose, Wisset Lodge, Hendham Road, Trinity Road, Upper Tooting, London, and did throw him down, and did beat him, and did murder him."

Corr-na-Fourin, by the way, was the spelling used in the transcription of the case, though the correct spelling was the

Lord Kingsburgh

one I have used, Coire-na-Fuaren. But what seemed odd in this indictment was that Laurie was not accused of robbing Rose, though an outsider might say that there was more evidence of Laurie having robbed Rose than having murdered him.

Fifteen good men and true (these were before the enlightened days when women were allowed to serve on a jury) were balloted. By the end of the first day of the trial the Laurie jury were complaining about the food that was served to them and the accommodation they had been given. The jury came from Edinburgh, Leith, Heriot, Biggar and Dalkeith, and they had to stay overnight in an Edinburgh hotel. I mention the food and the accommodation because I think they had an effect on the verdict, as had the telescoping of the trial into two days.

The trial's witnesses went over the story of Laurie and Rose as I have already told it. The prosecution's task was fairly straightforward, except, of course, that no one could prove that Laurie actually murdered Rose and so they had to depend on circumstantial evidence. The defence's task was even more difficult because Laurie insisted on the line of defence that he parted from Rose on the top of Goatfell, and never again set eyes on him, alive or dead. So the defence had to concentrate on persuading the jury that Rose's death was accidental.

The most important part of the trial was the medical evidence on what had happened to Rose and, as usual in murder trials, the doctors disagreed. Before that, however, there was a minor mystery of what had happened to Rose's boots? The three Arran policemen who were at the discovery of the body and supervised its journey to the coach house of the Corrie Hotel for the post-mortem were questioned at considerable length as to what had happened to the dead man's boots. They were not among the productions and the defence argued that they should have been because the state of the soles and the sprigs attached might give some idea of how Rose had met his death.

But the Arran police clammed up on this point. The sergeant and the two constables either gave evasive answers or no answers at all to the defence's questions. Two of them did say that they thought the boots were not important, and one of them eventually admitted that he had buried Rose's boots on the Corrie shore between the high and low water tidemarks. The defence, getting nowhere, abandoned that line of questioning. But the real reason that the boots were buried goes back to the fact that, even in Victorian days, Arran was still a Highland island, where a fair number of the inhabitants still spoke Arran Gaelic. And the Gaelic superstition was that, if a man met sudden death, his ghost would walk unless his boots were buried below the high water tidemark. When I first investigated this case one of the policemen, then retired, was still living and he was rather proud of his share in burying Rose's boots.

There was a difference of opinion on the difficulties or otherwise of descending the Gully of Springs. The defence made the most of its precipitous nature, but some of the witnesses for the prosecution, particularly the police, said that the descent on one side gave no trouble. The defence concentrated on two steep falls, one of 32 feet and one of nineteen feet. They also produced a witness who regarded the route Rose took as dangerous. He was Cosimo Latona, an Italian fisherman who lived in Corrie and described himself as a mountain guide. In cross-examination, however, he admitted he'd never guided anyone until after Rose's body was found.

Three eminent doctors gave it as their opinion that all Rose's injuries could have been caused by a fall – although it must be said that not one of them had actually seen the body. They were going on the medical evidence provided by the prosecution witnesses, who took the view that Rose had been

J. B. Balfour, counsel for the defence

attacked by someone wielding a large stone. Both sides admitted, however, that they could not absolutely disprove the other side.

But if Rose died as a result of a fall, how did various belongings of his come to be lying all over the Gully? How, in particular, did his cap come to be folded in four and placed under a big stone in the bed of a burn? And who was responsible for putting the body under a boulder and filling up the cavity with a barricade of stones, heather and moss? J. B. Balfour, the Dean of Faculty, who was Laurie's principal

The Solicitor-General

defence counsel, in reply then cast as big a slairt at Glasgow Fair holiday-makers as was ever thrown in Scotland.

"The Solicitor-General [for the prosecution]," said Mr. Balfour, "seems to think that we for the defence are admitting that Laurie robbed the body of Rose. We admit nothing of the kind. It may be that somebody did it. Very likely, at these Fair holidays, there would be plenty of people on the island who would do that."

A truly Edinburgh tribute to the Glasgow character!

On the second day of the trial the jury once again objected

to the dank air of the court, the poor meals served to them and the poor accommodation they were offered. It was pointed out to them by court officials that the Lord Justice-Clerk had said the trial must end by Saturday night, so they had only one more day to suffer!

On that Saturday night big crowds gathered outside newspaper offices and in the main streets of Glasgow, Greenock, Paisley, Hamilton, Coatbridge and a dozen other towns in the West of Scotland. They stood there silent, in their thousands, waiting for the verdict in the Arran murder trial. The general idea was that John Watson Laurie would be found Not Proven of the murder on Goatfell.

In the High Court of Edinburgh the Lord Justice-Clerk did not start his address to the jury until 8.40 p.m. William Roughead, the Edinburgh lawyer who became one of the most respected criminologists in the Western world, was in court and later wrote his account of the case. The judge's review of the evidence lasted exactly an hour and, said Roughead, "the packed audience hung upon his every word. Perhaps the most composed of his hearers was the accused, who looked steadfastly at the judge, with an occasional glance at the jury to see whether they appreciated certain judicial points."

The jury were out for three-quarters of an hour. When the bell rang to signify they had reached their verdict, and they filed back into their seats, not a juryman looked at the quiet, composed figure in the dock – a sure sign of the verdict to those accustomed to High Court trials.

The foreman rose. "The jury, by a majority, find the prisoner guilty", he announced. There was not the slightest sign of emotion from Laurie. But the judge, when he held the Black Cap above his head, spoke in a trembling voice as he sentenced Laurie to be hanged by the neck in the prison of Greenock. "This I pronounce for doom, and may the Lord have mercy on your soul."

As soon as the sentence was pronounced Laurie wheeled round in the dock, looked calmly over the crowded court and said, "Ladies and gentlemen, I am innocent of this charge."

"No one," wrote Roughead, "who witnessed the closing act of this famous trial can forget the impressive character of the scene. Without, in the black November night, a great crowd silently awaited the issue of life and death.

"The lofty, dimly-lighted Court room, the candles glimmering in the shadows of the Bench, the imposing presence of the Justice-Clerk in his robes of scarlet and white, the tiers of tense, expectant faces, and in the dock the cause and object of it all – the callous and brutal murderer whom Justice had tardily unmasked."

This is fine rodomontade, and doubtless William Roughead was convinced to the day he died that Laurie was a murderer. But the longer I have studied this case, the more inclined I am to the opinion that the Crown did not prove that Rose was murdered and that the jury's verdict should have been Not Proven, with Laurie going free.

Special editions of the newspapers were immediately rushed out, though it was now nearly 11 p.m. Police had to regulate the crowds round the street newsvendors and the newsagents' shops. At Hamilton the halfpenny papers were sold for fourpence each. John Watson Laurie would undoubtedly have been gratified if he had known of the interest displayed in his fate. But he had a quiet night in the Calton Jail in Edinburgh and was taken by train to Greenock next morning.

At Greenock he saw a small crowd on the platform and attempted to make a speech to them. But he was hustled off to the local jail, where he was to be hanged. A great gloom settled over Greenock, where there had not been a hanging since 1834.

As soon as the possibility of a reprieve was mentioned, the

inhabitants of Greenock rushed to support it. The movement for a petition to the Secretary for Scotland was started in Coatbridge, where Laurie's very respectable family lived. It had been found that the jury in Laurie's case had voted eight for Guilty and seven for Not Proven, and this narrowest of majorities was made one of the planks of the petition.

It was also asserted that the medical evidence was not conclusive, that there was insanity in Laurie's family, and that he had shown symptoms of mental aberration from infancy. By 22 November the organisers had 138,140 signatures, and a goodly proportion were from Greenock.

Some Doubting Thomases were more than a little doubtful about the petition. They suggested that Greenock people had signed it because they did not want the disgrace of a hanging in their town. One Letter to the Editor said that each signer should be made to sign over a sixpenny stamp and that would show the real worth of the petition. "I question very much," wrote another, "if ninety per cent of those who signed are not apprentices, office and message boys, servant girls and mill workers. With a few policemen knocking about, I'll be bound the petitions in this case wouldn't have come to much."

But there were influential people on Laurie's side too. One of them was the Assistant Physician to Glasgow Royal Infirmary, Dr. Campbell Black, who wrote several letters to the newspapers and then a pamphlet proving, to his and other people's satisfaction, that Rose had died as the result of a fall. Other doctors agreed with him, and there were some letters saying how easy it was to suffer from vertigo on a mountain side.

The Secretary for Scotland announced that a medical enquiry would be held to go into Laurie's mental condition. But there was no sign of a reprieve, and Greenock Town Council were forced to make arrangements for the hanging. They engaged Berry, the London hangman, and bought a flagpole and a black flag. The execution was fixed for 30 November, and the Town Council felt that there was no need to go to the expense of buying a scaffold. So they borrowed a scaffold from Glasgow and put it up behind the County Court buildings.

And what of Laurie in Greenock jail? At first he was as composed as he had been throughout the trial. When he heard, however, that his effigy was on show in a Glasgow Waxworks, he was very keen to see it and waxed wroth with the Governor because he was not given permission to visit Glasgow.

Laurie also wrote to the Secretary for Scotland. His letter admitted that he had not parted from Rose at the top of Goatfell after all. He now said that he had seen Rose fall from a high cliff and had gone to his assistance. By the time Laurie reached him, Rose was dead. He then rifled the dead man's pockets and buried the body.

There was no reply from the Secretary for Scotland and, two days before his execution was due, Laurie asked his warders how and to whom a confession should be made. But he never did make a confession, for that night the Secretary for Scotland issued an official statement: "In consequence of the Medical Commission having reported that the convict Laurie is of unsound mind, the Secretary for Scotland has felt justified in recommending that he should be respited."

On 1 December the Provost of Greenock received a telegram saying that the death sentence on Laurie had been commuted to penal servitude for life. Amid quiet rejoicing, the Greenockians took down the scaffold and sent it back to Glasgow. Later Greenock Town Council tried to recover the expenses they had paid for the scaffold, the flagpole and the flag, and the hiring of the hangman, but without success.

Greenock may have been happy about the cancellation of the hanging, but there were people in England who were not. One or two English newspapers went so far as to suggest that if it had been a Scotsman who was murdered by a Scotsman, and not an Englishman, the hanging would have been carried out.

A report was brought back from Greenock Prison about Laurie's behaviour there. "His references to Rose were not marked by any exhibition of sympathy for that unfortunate gentleman," said the report. "On the contrary, he spoke of him as a vain, proud man, always boastful of his money, and desirous of making his hearers believe that he was wealthy."

The significance of Laurie's comment upon this point is striking. With singular callousness he added that "Rose had not very much after all".

Poor Rose! If only he hadn't swanked about his money, he might have ended his life in the quietness of Brixton or Balham and had only pleasant memories of his holiday in Scotland.

On 2 December Laurie was transferred from Greenock to Perth Prison. All along the railway journey people somehow got to hear of Laurie's arrival and rushed to get a glimpse of the notorious Arran murderer. He seemed to have lost his taste for making speeches because this time he tried to hide from the crowds.

But he did not disappear from public ken. Fate had one or two strange tricks to play on him yet.

5

The unwanted man

John Watson Laurie was undoubtedly a person who desired, maybe above all things, to be the cynosure of neighbouring eyes. This is proved by his posturing in Rose's clothes after the unfortunate Englishman had disappeared, by his vainglorious Letters to the Editor, by his speech to the spectators when he has been found guilty of murder, by his anxiety to see his effigy in the Glasgow Waxworks, and by various attempts to address the public. His defence counsel's suggestion that he might plead insanity was turned down completely by Laurie, though his own defence that he had parted with Rose on the top of Goatfell was so patently untrue that it suggests that there was insanity in his make-up.

But people accused of murder hate the idea of insanity as far as they are concerned. The notorious mass murderer, Peter Manuel of Lanarkshire, is supposed to have killed at least sixteen persons – the full total may never be known. There was a suggestion that he might plead insanity. He not only rejected the idea but actually sacked the counsel for his defence, Lord Birsay, and conducted his own case. William Roughead, in his book on the trial of Laurie, suggests that it was just as well for the accused that he was not allowed to give evidence on his own behalf because he would probably have given himself away. Yet Manuel made a most spirited defence which surprised many people. But Roughead could be right, because Manuel was found guilty and hanged – the last hanging in Scotland, as it turned out.

I think it is worth while quoting William Roughead, a man for whom I have intense admiration except for one or two qualifications. In his *Trial of J. W. Laurie* he writes of the insanity plea that was first suggested in the petition which ended in the respite of Laurie and says, "That card [insanity] was first played by the petitioners and, as we have seen, it won the trick.

"But whether or not, and if so, to what extent Laurie, when he committed the crime, was technically insane, his behaviour exhibits certain well-marked features which I have noted as common to the many murderers whose conduct I have had occasion closely to study, from Mary Blandy in 1752 to Dr. Pritchard in 1865. None of these practitioners have, so far as I am aware, ever been deemed irresponsible or mentally deficient. All were liars, inveterate and gratuitous – the technical term is, I understand, 'pathological'; but their most striking characteristic is a supreme self-conceit and a total disregard for the claim to consideration of any one except themselves. Your murderer is the perfect egoist. For his especial benefit the sun shines daily, and the pick of the basket is his by right. This pleasant illusion is by the learned termed 'megalomania', and by the vulgar swollen head. It is not certifiable. A person of such importance cannot, of course, permit anybody else to get between him and the light or stand in the way of his desires. Should somebody do so, why then, so much the worse for somebody: he is liable to become, as our American friends would say, 'some' body."

Now, while I agree with Roughead's description of the perfect murderer, I do not agree that John Watson Laurie actually committed murder – or, at least, it was never proved that he did. Throughout his book Roughead refers to Laurie as "the murderer", sometimes "the callous murderer". To my mind the Crown did not prove that Laurie murdered Rose. The volume of medical opinion which was expressed at the end of the trial was quite definitely in favour of the theory that Rose died as the result of a fall from a height.

I first wrote about this strange case more than thirty years ago and, one way and another, I have been studying it ever since. What did happen in the Corrie of Springs? I think that Rose slipped and, by the time Laurie reached him, he was already dead or dying. A normal man would immediately have thought of trying to get help. Perhaps he would have struggled back up to the summit of the mountain in the hope that other climbers had arrived there. At any rate, he would have tried to do something.

But Laurie was not a normal man. He must have thought about the position he was in for some time. Then, and only a person of limited intelligence could have done this, he turned out Rose's pockets and took what he wanted. Now, of course, he could not leave the body to be discovered and he saw the convenient boulder. It must have taken a long time for him to get the body into its hiding place, and even longer to close up the gap with boulders, stones, heather and moss. Some of the boulders were very big. And then, with his booty, Laurie descended the mountain by Glen Sannox to Corrie.

When Rose's body was discovered and the search for the mysterious John Annandale was going on, you may recollect that Laurie met his friend Aitken for a second time in Glasgow and, when Aitken asked him, "Whose cap were you wearing that Friday when I met you in Rothesay?", Laurie gasped, "Surely you don't think I am a . . .?" Aitken thought he was going to add the word "thief". Then Laurie hastily departed the scene.

I think this is significant, because Laurie knew he was a thief. Equally, he knew he was not a murderer, so he had nothing to deny there. Some students of this case might take the view that the missing word was "murderer". Surely the observant Aitken would see how Laurie's lips were moving, and the consonant "m" for murderer is shaped entirely differently from "th" for thief. Try saying the words yourself if you don't believe me.

Of all the comments on the trial I like best that which appeared in the Scottish Leader on 19 November, about two weeks before the Secretary for Scotland recommended that Laurie should be respited. An article in this magazine ran, "The movement to obtain a reprieve for the Arran murderer has very quickly acquired great force. In this there is much significance, because Laurie's case makes no adventitious calls upon sympathy such was was noticeable in the Maybrick trial. On the contrary, the whole circumstances of the Arran tragedy are of an especially forbidding type, the work, so far as we may venture to judge, of a peculiarly callous nature on which sympathy would be wasted.

"It may therefore be taken that in regard to Laurie there are special features which drive out of mind the unalloyed repulsiveness of the murder and impel men to ask mercy for him. In these columns protest against capital punishment has always been made on the broad ground of principle. We have argued that the practice of hanging has no real deterrent effect. Those whose low moral instincts permit them to take life have not the wit to be in dread of the hangman. What society has to do, then, is to deal with the dwarfed human types in a spirit, not of revenge, but of pity, and to take care that they are rendered powerless for further evil.

"What society unhappily does as a rule is to take upon itself the responsibility for the public executioner, and the burden of the acts of a functionary who, despite the social service he is supposed to be rendering, is regarded as rather worse that an outcast, fitted only to break the necks of fellow creatures in its name. On no ground of reason or morals can this be defended, and the practice is persisted in simply because the ideas and sentiments relating to it are not analysed. We are barbarous indeed with the words of civilisation on our lips.

"But in addition to the general reasons for asking clemency for Laurie there are very special reasons more or less apparent to all who consider the circumstances. In the first place, there is the uncertainty dwelling in men's minds as to whether an act literally to be described as murder was actually perpetrated; the dubiety arising from the absence of intelligent motive. There was no passion in the case; the association of the two men was accidental and unsought by Laurie; and all the hope of wealth that was held out cannot be conceived as tempting anyone but an insane creature to an act so atrocious. If murder were done, then within Laurie's nature there is enclosed a psychological enigma which the general human experience is powerless to explain.

"In the second place, those who are bestirring themselves in the interests of the prisoner are entitled to plead that the trial was unduly hurried. It was, doubtless, with the best of motives that Lord Kingsburgh announced his determination to finish the case within two days; but when men are solemnly contemplating the extinction of life this determination to rush matters has an ugly look. Men are asking what the practical effect of it could have been on the minds of the jury.

"Fifteen citizens were in durance for two days. They were on their own showing but indifferently supplied with food and refreshment. Late on Saturday night, when called upon to give the verdict, they must have been worn out with the strain, excitement, and long confinement in bad air. In short, the whole conditions were such as to prevent men from bringing their faculties into full and vital activity on the evidence regarding which they had to form so grave a judgment. Without at this moment questioning their judgment in the least, we have no hesitation in saying that the fifteen jurymen were of jaded minds, and it is not to men in such a condition that the issue of life or death should be entrusted.

"In the third place, there is a powerful reason for staying the hand of the executioner in the fact that the verdict was only obtained by a majority of one vote. The recourse, to the ballot, as it happens, was an irregularity which the jury would probably not fallen into had there been no pressure upon them to close the case. It has been so far profitable, however, as to show us by what proportion of the jury Laurie's life has been declared forfeit. The division of opinion revealed makes the infliction of the capital sentence a matter of deeper solemnity. It may be a defect in the law that no verdict was possible save that which either condemned or liberated Laurie; but it is horrible beyond expression to think that for this man absolute freedom and a criminal's death was determined by the vote of a single fagged-out juryman. Surely in a case so surrounded with difficulties, and when the deliberations of the jury so nearly came to the point of breaking down, the right, the reasonable, and the humane course is to take the side of leniency.

"There are too many people in society, unfortunately, who can divest themselves of all responsibility for the law, thinking that when the matter has been taken out of their hands it moves along by some perfect machinery which it is presumptuous to question; but the great majority of citizens, we feel sure, will breathe all the more freely when they know that legalised murder is not to be done in their name on grounds so dubious."

I have given the Scottish Leader's statement in full because I think it is the last word on the trial. As a High Court reporter for my newspaper I have seen several men condemned to be hanged. Thank God, I have never seen a woman so sentenced. The people who talk about bringing back hanging are either over-emotional or just as callous as anyone who takes another person's life. Few, apart perhaps for some police officers, have witnessed a hanging. I knew a bright, clever business man in Glasgow who became a Town Councillor and then a Bailie. As he was the Junior Bailie it was his duty to attend a hanging at Duke Street Prison. He never recovered from the experience. His health and his business suffered and he died only a few years later. This is sober fact and I use the adjective advisedly because the story should surely have a sobering effect on those who demand the return of this obscene punishment.

Back to John Watson Laurie. It's indicative of his completely irresponsible state of mind that in Perth Prison he was jubilant about the result of the petition. His own estimation, discussing his case with the warders, was that he would be released after two years. But, for once, the new sentence of penal servitude for life worked out exactly as it implied. It was carried out to the letter and Laurie died at the age of 66 still in prison.

The convicted man went to Perth Prison in December, 1889 at the age of 25, and he was later transferred to the grim Peterhead Penitentiary in the far North of Scotland. The Secretary for Scotland had stated that he had commuted the sentence of death because of Laurie's mental state. But in Peterhead he did not seem so very different from the other convicts. He was inclined to be surly, and was forever annoying the Governor and others in authority with elaborate complaints which turned out to be groundless.

On the other hand, he was a good worker and showed how well he had been trained in the Atlas Engineering Works in Springburn before he went for his ill-starred holiday to Rothesay at the Fair. Laurie claimed to be religious and the chaplain at Peterhead eventually appointed him to the important post of precentor in the prison chapel. In those days there was still a strong feeling against organ music in the Scottish churches – an organ was dismissed as a "kist o' whistles". A precentor was preferred and the precentor was equipped with a tuning fork. After the minister had announced the next psalm, the precentor would sound the appropriate note with his tuning fork and then lead the congregation in praise. Laurie had a good, strong voice and was regarded as one of the best precentors that Peterhead Prison had had.

One way and another, Laurie worked himself up to the position of first-class prisoner, with attendant privileges. In the early morning of 24 July 1893, he was one of a gang of prisoners erecting a scaffolding in front of a new block of houses for prison officers. About 7.45 a dense sea fog (what they call on the East coast a "haar") came down over Peterhead and visibility was limited to less than a hundred yards.

Laurie was carrying a long plank towards the scaffolding when he suddenly made a dash for a nearby wall. He placed the plank against the wall and was over in a twinkling. He ran across the Aberdeen road and leapt over a dyke into a field of clover.

As he crossed the road, Laurie was seen by an armed guard watching from a sentry box on the prison wall. The guard aimed and fired, but his carbine apparently jammed. By the time he had reloaded, Laurie had disappeared into the haar.

The alarm sounded at once and a number of warders and civil guards gave chase. The escaped convict crossed three dykes and saw what he thought was a wood ahead of him. It was just behind a wee house called Bellevue Cottage, and he made for the trees with the warders blowing warning whistles behind him. When the inhabitants of Bellevue heard the whistling, they hastily locked their doors and bolted their windows. They had suffered escapes before.

Just as Laurie was approaching the trees the sun pierced the sea fog. One warder had mounted his bicycle and was speeding along the main road when he suddenly saw Laurie reach what the escaper hoped was a hiding place. But it turned out to be merely a small plantation and the warder jumped off his bike and grappled with the convict.

Laurie put up a fight, but other warders came on the scene and he was soon being led back to Peterhead, using language that a precentor should never have even known, far less spoken. He must have been particularly disgusted to realise that this was the second time he had trusted to a wood, and it had failed him.

His punishment in Peterhead Prison was to have an iron belt riveted round his waist, and this belt was attached by heavy chains to iron anklets. He had to wear these ornaments day and night for some time. Some years ago I did an investigative tour of Scottish prisons and when I visited Peterhead I saw that belt and chains. They were still used on escapees when they were brought back.

No more was heard of John Watson Laurie for sixteen years. Then in 1909 rumours appeared in some newspapers that he had been released after spending twenty years in prison. These rumours were just rumours, and the first real news of Laurie appeared in the Daily Record on 27 April 1910.

"The Arran Murderer at Perth" was the Record's headline and the report read: "The murder of the English excursionist, Edwin Robert Rose, on the slopes of Goatfell, Arran, over twenty years ago was recalled yesterday by the removal of Laurie, who was convicted of the crime, from Peterhead penal establishment to the Perth Criminal Asylum.

"It does not necessarily follow that because Laurie has been removed to Perth Criminal Asylum that his mental condition has prompted the transfer. On this point the officials approached refused to speak."

I must point out, however, that it was later discovered that Laurie had been officially certified as suffering from progressive dementia.

"Laurie was removed in company with five other convicts,"

the Record went on. "The tragic party left Peterhead in charge of three warders at half-past nine in the morning and travelled in a specially reserved compartment. Laurie was easily distinguished. The Arran murderer, however, has aged considerably. His hair, cropped close in accordance with prison rules, is quite grey, and his face is wan and haggard. He walks with a stoop, and his whole appearance points to his being in the latest stages of senile decay."

This seems a remarkable description of one who was only 45, and it must be said that the photograph does not agree with the reporter. Laurie looks a sturdy figure, and his head is obviously bowed in an attempt to defeat the photographer.

Now this episode of 1910, according to most devotees of the Arran murder mystery, is the last anyone heard of John Watson Laurie until he died on 5 October 1930. But when I did my first investigations into the Laurie case in the summer of 1955, I was also moving about the Firth of Clyde seeing the summer shows. At the Barrfields Pavilion in Largs the stars were Grace Clark and Colin Murray, famous in Scotland as "Mr. and Mrs. Glasgow".

I had written a little about the Goatfell mystery and, when I met Gracie and Colin behind the scenes at Barrfields, they wanted to tell me their Laurie story. It went back to 1928, when Colin was the baritone and Gracie the pianist of a concert party appearing in Perth. They'd just met for the first time.

While the show was on the company were asked to give a concert in Perth Prison. Concerts are held in the chapel of the prison and, when I saw it on my prison tour, the hall looked much the same as it was in 1928 – with one exception. My view took in a good sized stage. There was no stage in 1928, only a sort of verandah or minstrels' gallery, which stuck out of the wall a goodly distance above the audience.

The hall itself was divided by a barricade. The ordinary prisoners occupied one side, and the inmates from the

Criminal Lunatic Department were on the other. The concert party were up in the minstrels' gallery and, as they looked down at the prisoners, both Colin and Gracie noticed a silver-haired, rosy-cheeked old man sitting in the front row on the Lunatic side. "He was one of the nicest-looking old chaps I've ever seen," Colin Murray told me.

It was announced that Colin would sing "The Standard on the Braes o' Mar", and Gracie played the opening bars. As Colin cleared his throat, a man on the Lunatic side suddenly rose and, as Colin launched into the first line, he did the same. Verse for verse, word for word, he sang right through the song!

When the concert ended this singer suddenly rose again and said, "Ladies and gentlemen, I will now ask my old friend, John Laurie, for to propose a vote of thanks."

The old man in the front row hung his head and soon the prison officers were ushering the convicts out. Colin and Gracie turned to the Governor of the prison and asked if this handsome old man was really the famous Arran murderer.

The Governor said he was. "Well," said Colin, "he doesn't look in the least mad to me."

The Governor didn't answer that one, but he did explain that Laurie was kept in Perth after 39 years in prison because nobody wanted him and he had nowhere to go. While this casts a certain reflection on his family, there is another side to the situation. It is well known that some men gradually regard prison as their home. They feel safe there. I recollect the case of a man found guilty of murdering his wife, who was so quiet and inoffensive that the authorities decided that he should be moved to an Open Prison. He was a very small man and had been completely dominated by a big, overbearing woman who was an alcoholic. On one occasion he could stand his wife's berating no longer, lifted a handy axe and killed her. The general opinion was that he had been provoked so much and so often that it was not surprising that he had eventually rebelled – even so conclusively.

When this Scottish Open Prison had first been mooted, there was intense disfavour for the scheme among the inhabitants of the nearby town. They were opposed to long-term criminals being deposited in their midst, but eventually agreement was reached with the local people that no person guilty of violence would be housed in the Open Prison.

It was discovered in the town that a man convicted of murdering his wife had arrived in the prison, and was therefore entitled to walk about the district without let or hindrance. All hell was let loose. But the problem was quickly solved. The Governor of the Open Prison had a talk with the murderer, who confessed that he was completely miserable under his new conditions. Indeed, it seemed that he suffered from a sort of agoraphobia and couldn't stand the thought of going out in the open. He told the Governor that he would only be happy when he was returned from the closed prison, whence he had come. So he was returned to his own wee cell and everybody lived happily ever after.

John Watson Laurie did not suffer from agoraphobia. The Governor of Perth Prison called him in to his office one day and told him that he was now so trusted that he would be allowed out of his cell to walk about Perth almost any time he felt like it. There must have been some restrictions, but many people in the town could have seen this pleasant-looking, white-haired old man wandering around the streets of Perth about the years 1927 to 1930 and never suspected for a moment that he had been the central figure of one of the most notorious murder trials in Scotland.

I wonder if Laurie, as he strolled his benign way round Perth, ever gave a thought to that grave in Glen Sannox kirkyard with the inscription carved on the mountain boulder above it – "In loving memory of Edwin R. Rose, who died on Goatfell, 15th July, 1889."

THE ARDLAMONT MYSTERY

Ardlamont House

1

Sad shooting accident at Ardlamont

You won't find in the whole world a more beautiful setting for a murder than Ardlamont Estate on the Kyles of Bute. The Kyles are one of the glories of Scotland, a country full of glories. You can reach Tighnabruaich, the capital of the Kyles, by road and by cruising steamer, but in Victorian days most people reached it by the ubiquitous paddler. Don't worry about the name, by the way. Tighnabruaich is the Gaelic for "House on the hill". This part of the Firth of Clyde abounds in Gaelic names, for the Lamonts, a famous Highland Clan, were in possession hereabouts, until the Campbells of Argyll swept them out.

Ardlamont House was at the foot of the peninsula, overlooking Ardlamont Bay and the entrance to Loch Fyne. It was a very handsome building indeed – I should say "is" because it is still there, but you can see it only on a cruise up Loch Fyne to Inveraray, the home, incidentally, of the Duke of Argyll, Chief of Clan Campbell. From the deck you can see the imposing frontage of Ardlamont House, looking towards the mountains of Arran where Rose and Laurie played out their strange tragedy.

Here, across the sparkling waters of the Clyde, another strange tragedy was enacted. On the afternoon of 10 August 1893, a small paragraph appeared in the Glasgow Evening

News. It read –

SAD SHOOTING ACCIDENT AT
ARDLAMONT

Young Man Killed
(From Our Own Correspondent)

Greenock, 1.30 – News has been received from Greenock today of a sad gun accident which took place at Ardlamont on Loch Fyne yesterday. The report is that yesterday afternoon a young man, 21 years of age, named Hamburgh, who lately came from America, was out shooting on his estate only recently acquired when, as he was going over a dyke, his gun accidentally went off and he was fatally wounded.

There were two small mistakes in this report. The victim's name was Cecil Hambrough and he had never been in America. There could also be an argument as to whether he had, in fact, "recently acquired" the estate. But the newspaper was not to know that – they were depending on a rather garbled 'phone call from Tighnabruaich.

Later reports in the Scottish newspapers were more factual. Cecil Hambrough, they said, came of a well-to-do family in the south of England. He was the guest at Ardlamont House of a Mr. A. J. Monson, who had taken the shooting for the season, and whose steam yacht, *Alert,* was at Tighnabruaich. It seemed to be one of those sad accidents which came along with every shooting season in Scotland. Newspaper readers scanned the paragraphs, had a momentary pang of sympathy for the dead man and his family, and passed on to something else in the paper.

One person who did not see the Evening News story of 10 August was a reporter on the Evening News. His name was Neil Munro and he was to become not only Editor of the

Lieutenant Hambrough

News, but one of Scotland's most renowned authors. His novels, such as *The New Road, Children of the Mist* and *Doom Castle*, were famous and under the name of "Hugh Foulis" he wrote the "Para Handy" books, still popular today and the subject of several nation-wide television series. He did not read the paragraph in the News because he happened to be on holiday at his home town, Inveraray, and it took quite a while for the papers to get there in those days.

On the evening of the day after the shooting accident report appeared, Neil Munro met his friend, Tom Macnaughton, at Inveraray. Macnaughton was Depute Fiscal of Argyll and he was newly back from a professional visit to Ardlamont. He told Neil Munro about the shooting, which he had gone to investigate, and said that Cecil Hambrough's host, Mr. Monson, had been so upset by the affair that he refused to look again at the corpse which he had discovered.

Indeed, the Depute Fiscal himself had to help to dress the dead body because Mr. Monson could not bring himself to perform that last duty to his young friend. But Mr. Macnaughton seemed now to be just as upset as had Mr. Monson. All of a sudden he said to Neil Munro, "I've very grave doubts about the character of that accident." And then he shut up like a clam, and wouldn't say another word about Ardlamont.

A few days later came the end of Neil Munro's holiday. He was 29 and one of those reporters who were given special assignments, because he was considered keen and a fine descriptive writer. On holiday he wasn't thinking in the least of news stories but before he left Inveraray on his return to Glasgow he went to see an official of the County Court there. It so happened that this official was also local correspondent for the Evening News and Munro said to him, "If the police decide to take any action about the accident at Ardlamont, wire me at the Glasgow office."

Several more days elapsed and Neil Munro was beginning

Alfred John Monson

to think that his friend Macnaughton's suspicions were groundless, when a telegram arrived at the News office. It was from Inveraray and it said cryptically, "Go to Ardlamont."

Neil Munro lost no time. In a few hours he was landing on Auchenlochan pier, which was the nearest pier to Ardlamont (in Victorian days there were four piers almost within sight of each other; there is only Tighnabruaich pier now). He saw a policeman on the pier and asked how far it was to Ardlamont House. The policeman told him and added, "You'll be the insurance company?" Neil Munro just left him with that impression and crossed to the Auchenlochan Hotel, where he hired a horse and trap to take him the five miles to Ardlamont. He knew that this would have to be a quick job if he was to get the last steamer back to Glasgow.

Up the road to Ardlamont trotted the horse. Neil Munro saw the white front of the Georgian house with the lawn in front and the thick woods all round. The atmosphere on that August afternoon was anything but murderous. The wood-pigeons were cooing among the trees and there wasn't a soul about. After a while he discovered the factor, a Mr. Steven. He gave Munro all the details he could. According to Steven there wasn't the slightest doubt that it was an accident.

Although it was a dark and stormy morning on 10 August, young Cecil Hambrough had gone out shooting with Mr. Monson and a chap called Scott. They had started at the schoolhouse, just below Ardlamont House, and entered the wood on the right. Hambrough and Monson were carrying guns but Scott had no gun. He was there to carry what they shot.

Hambrough entered the wood to the right and Monson to the extreme left. Scott was farther back and in the centre. Monson and Scott lost sight of Hambrough, they said. Then they heard a shot and Monson cried, "Have you got any-thing?" When there was no reply from Hambrough, they went through the wood and found him lying beside a dyke, dead or dying.

That was the story which Monson had told Steven, and which Steven now told Neil Munro. He added that Mr. Monson was out shooting on the hill with some of the dead man's fellow officers from the Yorkshire Militia. If Mr. Munro would like to wait until the shooting was over, he could have a personal interview with Mr. Monson. To Neil Munro's eternal regret, he refused this offer. He was thinking of the last steamer to Glasgow. He thanked the factor, got into his gig and the horse spanked its way down to Auchenlochan pier, just as the handsome *Lord of the Isles* came in from

Inveraray on her way back to Glasgow. He'd just caught his steamer and no more.

Two gangways were thrown between the pier and the steamer, one for those who wanted to embark and the other for those who were disembarking. As Neil Munro went up one, he saw descending the other the Chief Constable of Argyll and several Sheriff Court officials he knew by sight in Inveraray. That was enough – his story was complete.

"The Ardlamont Mystery" was the title he gave to his scoop in the Evening News next day. And it was such a scoop that it didn't only surprise the other Glasgow newspapers. It even surprised, and horrified, the Crown Authorities in Edinburgh, who had never received a detailed report from the Argyll police and had already written off the case as a simple shooting accident.

And, ere you criticise the Procurator Fiscal and the Chief Constable of Argyll, you must remember that in those Good Old Days no one thought of questioning the motives of a well-dressed Englishman, who took over the big estate, bought a steam yacht, engaged a butler and a staff of eight, ordered wine and whisky by the case, and generally conducted himself as such Superior Beings did when they condescended to take a shooting in Scotland for the season.

Even on 23 August, a fortnight after Cecil Hambrough's death, the Procurator Fiscal of Argyll did not know that Monson had insured Cecil Hambrough for £20,000 – just two days before he was found shot! By 30 August, however, the Argyll authorities felt they were justified in taking certain steps. The Sheriff-Substitute went from Inveraray to Ardlamont, presented a warrant to an apparently astounded Mr. Monson, and proceeded to search the house for papers.

When the Sheriff carried out the unpleasant duty, to a gentleman, of having to search Mrs. Monson's room, he came across a private drawer in which was a bundle of documents. Mrs. Monson was present, of course. She was a good-looking, rather aristocratic lady and she had three small children. When the Sheriff opened the private drawer Mrs. Monson asked him to give her two letters from that bundle. Tears came to her eyes as she pleaded for these letters, which she said were private and personal. The Sheriff was as susceptible to the tyranny of tears as any man. He handed the letters over to Mrs. Monson, and they were never seen again. What effect they might have had on the trial of Mrs. Monson's husband we can only imagine.

Not long after the Sheriff had given Mrs. Monson her two letters back, and sealed the rest of the documents for future use, Mr. Alfred John Monson himself was driving along the road between Ardlamont and Tighnabruaich. He saw a carriage approaching and somebody signalling him to stop. So he did and out of the carriage stepped the Chief Constable of Argyll. "Alfred John Monson," he said, "I have to arrest you on the charge of murdering Cecil Hambrough."

2

Dramatis personae

How did Monson, Cecil and the mysterious Mr. "Scott", come to be together in the Ardlamont woods on that dark, stormy August morning?

Let's take the victim first. Windsor Dudley Cecil Hambrough was only 20 when he was shot dead at Ardlamont. He was a lieutenant in the Yorkshire Militia and he had been "tutored" for the Army by A. J. Monson since he was seventeen. He was six feet-something tall, rather harum-scarum, and he didn't have much in the way of brains. He was so completely under Monson's domination that some people said afterwards that Monson was a hypnotist and kept Cecil Hambrough in a more or less constant trance.

Young Hambrough was the son and heir of a Major Dudley Hambrough, the scion of a very rich family who had left him estates which brought him in not less than £4000 a year, an immense amount in Victorian days. But £4000 a year wasn't nearly enough for Major Hambrough. It's true he was not a well man, but he seemed also to have a positive gift for throwing money away. In 1885 he'd got £37,000 from the Eagle Insurance Company by mortgaging his life interest. But he went through that £37,000 in less than five years and was more or less penniless in 1890.

This tragic spendthrift and his wife were forced to leave

one home after another, and at last were living in third-rate
digs in London. Even then they had to keep moving from one
mean place to another to avoid the Major's many creditors.
And at the same time Major Hambrough was arranging to
send his two daughters to be educated in Germany!

One of the financiers (or money-lenders, if you want a
blunter term) who was helping Major Hambrough and trying
to get him more money from his already mortgaged estates
was a Londoner with the resounding name of Beresford
Loftus Tottenham, known as "Tot" to his friends. He was
lending money to the Major in the hope that he'd get it all
back with interest some day. "Tot" was an imposing military
figure even in civilian clothes. He was just over thirty and had
served in the 10th Hussars. Later he joined the Turkish Army
and took part in the suppression of the Cretan insurrection of
1889. Today we would call him a "mercenary". At any rate, he
made enough money out of his Turkish escapade to be able
to start a London financial firm to which he gave the name of
Kempton and Co.

Major Hambrough wanted his son Cecil to go into the
Army, so "Tot" introduced the Major to a Mr. A. J. Monson,
who was prepared to act as tutor to the boy for the sum of
£300 a year. Nobody ever explained what qualifications A. J.
Monson had for the job.

But the Major, as a gentleman, knew another gentleman
when he saw one, and Monson was obviously aristocratic. He
was tall and slim, with a pale clean-cut face, yellow hair and
what William Roughead, who later saw him in the dock,
described as "strange, shifty eyes". He was, needless to say,
well groomed and quite boyish looking for his thirty years.

Monson soon let the Major know that the "tutor" he had
engaged had family ties with Lord Houghton and Lord
Crewe, and that his uncle, Sir Edmund John Monson, was the
British Ambassador in Vienna – all of which was perfectly
true. He had been educated at Rugby and Oxford, and went

out as a Government official to South Africa. In Capetown he married Agnes Maud, the daughter of a Yorkshire colliery owner, but later he got tired of South Africa and brought his wife back to England. He told the Major that he was just giving up his house at the Woodlands, near Harrogate, and moving to Riseley Hall in Yorkshire.

What poor old Major Hambrough didn't know about this gentlemanly tutor he'd engaged to look after his son was that Monson was living on his wits and was about to be made bankrupt. He was, like John Watson Laurie, the black sheep of the family, albeit that his family were on a higher social scale than Laurie's. Soon after he returned from South Africa, he leased a large mansion called Cheyney Court. He insured this house against fire, and a few weeks later it was burnt to the ground.

Monson collected the insurance and moved his family to Gaddesley Farm. There he was involved in various agricultural transactions which ended in his being tried for fraud. He was acquitted, but felt it wise to move again. And, just as he was introduced to Major Hambrough, he was still living in Harrogate. Young Cecil went to live at the Woodlands, and was immensely impressed by the scale on which his new tutor lived. Monson kept hunters, gave little dinners to all the nobs in the district, and lived the life of a lord. He was also overdrawing his bank account and running up enormous bills in hotels and shops all over Yorkshire.

I dare say that Cecil Hambrough was rather surprised when his apparently wealthy tutor was declared bankrupt. But no doubt Monson had a good excuse. At any rate, his liabilities were £56,000 and his assets £600, and right to the end of his days he remained an undischarged bankrupt.

Life in Harrogate wasn't quite so pleasant now that he'd been declared bankrupt. He didn't like the hurt looks which the hotelkeepers and the tradesmen were giving him. So he went to Riseley Hall, his eleventh home since returning from

South Africa. Apparently no one there knew he was a bankrupt, for soon he was living in as fine a style as ever.

He engaged a butler, a governess for his children, a coachman, various servants and outdoor hands, and a tutor for Cecil Hambrough at £150 a year. No one seems to have thought it was at all strange that a tutor should engage a tutor to do his tutoring for him. Certainly Major Hambrough wouldn't object, because about this time he was meeting Monson occasionally in London and Monson often gave him a couple of sovereigns, just to keep the wolf from the door.

Why should Monson do this? Because he had set his heart on acquiring the great Hambrough estates. He was going to do this by buying Major Hambrough's life interest from the Eagle Insurance Company. You may wonder how an undischarged bankrupt was going to manage this, but Monson was an expert in the labyrinthine ways of finance. If he could get hold of the Hambrough estates and also control young Cecil, who would be 21 in 1894, then a beautiful new life would unfold before him, and he'd never need to worry about money again.

So life was merry and bright at Riseley Hall, although Agnes Maud Monson was later to describe it in a weekly magazine as "unbearable". But that was, apparently, because she didn't like the way her husband held drinking parties almost every night. Drink had no effect whatever on Monson, but he liked to see other people "under the influence". Once, when she protested, Monson attacked his wife. But young Cecil Hambrough came to her rescue. Monson apologised and all seemed forgiven and forgotten.

But things were not at all well behind the scenes. Monson was as deep in debt as ever. It was then that he decided to go to Scotland for a change of air, and he fixed on Ardlamont, where that ancient Scottish family, the Lamonts of Cowal, were offering the estate for sale at a price of £85,000. Mr. Monson let it be understood that he would probably buy, but in the meantime he'd take the shooting for the season at a rent of £450. And that was how the Monson family and Cecil Hambrough came to be at Ardlamont House.

Although Alfred John Monson had no money of his own, he had two "friends" who were supporting him and knew of his plans for getting hold of the Hambrough estates. One we have already met – the odd Mr. Beresford Loftus Tottenham ("Tot" to his friends) and an equally odd London character who called himself Mr. Adolphus Frederick James Jerningham. "Tot" was already sending young Cecil £10 a week just to keep him going, and £10 was a lot of money in those days, when you were considered well off indeed if you made £5 a week.

Monson's troubles were compounded when Major Dudley Hambrough decided in April 1893, that he wasn't having anything more to do with A. J. Monson. Not only that, but he started to persuade his son to leave Monson and return to the bosom of the Hambrough family. What had incensed the Major was that he had insisted that Cecil should go into the Hampshire Militia, in which he had a number of good friends who could be depended on to help the boy, but Monson had entered Cecil for the Yorkshire Militia. It was pretty obvious that Monson had done this so as to keep Cecil in Yorkshire while he was staying at Riseley Hall.

No matter how much Major Hambrough implored his son to return, Cecil was adamant about staying with Monson. Maybe it was only natural that he preferred the high life of the Monson establishment to the low digs in London which Major and Mrs. Hambrough were forced to occupy.

So the situation with Alfred John Monson in the summer of 1893 was that he had lost his hold on the Hambrough estates, but he still had his hold on Cecil Hambrough. He was deeply in debt at Riseley Hall when he negotiated to take over the shooting at Ardlamont for a rent of £450 for the season. This was to be paid on 1 August, and at the beginning of July

Monson moved his wife, family and Cecil Hambrough from Riseley Hall to Ardlamont House.

He got Beresford Loftus Tottenham to advance him enough money to take his party from Yorkshire to Argyll, but he had to leave all the family linen in the local laundry because he couldn't afford to pay for it.

When the Monsons arrived at Ardlamont, the aristocratic gentleman had only half-a-crown in his pocket. That was his entire capital, because he had not only spent the money which "Tot" had loaned him, but also the money which Mrs. Monson had got by pawning various pieces of silver and her personal jewellery. Indeed, when it came to the trial of A. J. Monson for the murder of Cecil Hambrough, no fewer than five pawn tickets were among the official productions in the case.

But no one in Scotland knew of Mr. Monson's difficulties. The Scots accepted him at his face value, and that was a high one. He was the shooting tenant at Ardlamont Estate and that was enough to get him unlimited credit. So he had his butler and his staff, his food and wine, and even "bought" the steam yach *Alert,* which lay at Tighnabruaich awaiting his command. He also allowed it to be understood that he would be buying Ardlamont – though the price was £85,000 and he had only 2s 6d towards it.

Exactly one month before Cecil Hambrough was shot dead in Ardlamont woods, A. J. Monson tried to negotiate a £50,000 policy on Cecil's life – in his wife's name, of course, because Monson was a great believer in doing everything in his wife's name. But the canny Scottish Provident Institution in Edinburgh wanted to know what Mrs. Monson's interest was in Cecil's life, so Monson cut the sum to £10,000. The Edinburgh office still wanted to know Mrs. Monson's interest, so Monson turned to the Liverpool and London and Globe Company.

This company were ready to give insurance for £50,000 if

Mrs. Monson's interest in Cecil's life was revealed, so now Monson did another cut and fixed the sum at £26,000. He sent the company a letter signed by Cecil Hambrough. It was dated 31 July 1893, from Ardlamont House and young Hambrough wrote – "I am requested by Mrs. Agnes Monson to write and inform you that she has an interest in my life to the extent of £26,000. I have given her an undertaking under which I agree to pay her this sum after my attaining twenty-one, if I should live till then."

The last six words are the most interesting part of this letter. But the Liverpool and London and Globe were having none of it, and on 2 August Monson called at the Glasgow office of the Mutual Assurance Company of New York with an entirely new story. Now he explained that he was the guardian of Cecil Hambrough, who was coming into a fortune of £200,000. Cecil was about to buy Ardlamont Estate and Mrs. Monson was advancing £20,000 to Cecil for this project. The boy's life was to be insured for £20,000 to cover this advance. Monson was most insistent that all arrangements should be made by 8 August, as that was the date when Ardlamont was to be bought.

The insurance manager believed him and Monson brought Cecil Hambrough along that very afternoon to be medically examined and then to sign the proposal forms for two policies of £10,000 each. The premium was to be £194 3s 4d. How could a man with no money pay a premium of nearly £200? Nothing was impossible to A. J. Monson! He wrote to his old pal "Tot" and explained that he was going to buy Ardlamont Estate for Cecil Hambrough. The price was £48,000 and the deposit would be £250. He'd told Cecil that the price was actually £50,000, so that there would be £1000 each for Beresford Loftus Tottenham and Alfred John Monson.

There wasn't a word of truth in this, but "Tot" liked the idea of making an easy thousand and sent his cheque (to Mrs.

Monson, of course) for £250. Mrs. Monson had already opened an account at the Royal Bank of Scotland, Tighnabruaich, with £15, a transaction which the Royal Bank were bitterly to regret. On 8 August Monson paid the premium of £194 3s 4d to the Mutual Assurance Company of New York.

It's obvious that Agnes Maud Monson and Cecil Hambrough were puppets who obeyed their master's command, and the master, of course, was Alfred John Monson. Earlier in this fateful year of 1893 Mrs. Monson, officially, had brought an action against the Monson pupil, Cecil Hambrough for £1000 for board, lodging and education. The suit, you may be surprised to know, was undefended and Mrs. Monson got the judgment of the court. She never collected the money. Her husband sold the £1000 judgment to his friend "Tot" for £200 ready cash.

Cecil Hambrough agreed with everything that his tutor told him. So here he was, a big, happy lump of a boy, having a wonderful holiday at Ardlamont and looking forward to the arrival of three of his particular officer pals in the Yorkshire Militia for the "Glorious Twelfth". Alas, there was to be an inglorious tenth of August first of all. Incidentally, it must be remarked that the invitation to Cecil's fellow officers would please Cecil's tutor because they would pay for the privilege of staying in Ardlamont House and shooting over Ardlamont Estate.

And now that the £20,000 insurance on Cecil was fixed, the ingenious Mr. Monson asked a friend from London to join them at Ardlamont. The more the merrier, you might say. This friend was a bookie's clerk named Ted Davis – hardly the type you'd expect to find as a guest in a mansion house with a butler and all the trimmings. Ted Davis arrived at Ardlamont and was introduced as "Mr. Scott".

It should be said that Cecil Hambrough was Monson's pupil in every sense of the word, and the kindly tutor had often taken the heir to the Hambrough estates round the "racing" hotels and pubs of London when, in Monson's own fine phrase, he was trying to make some oof from the gee-gees. Monson knew some very peculiar people indeed, and he was now about to thrust unwanted fame on one of them – the bookie's clerk who was sometimes known as Edward Sweeney, sometimes as Edward Davis and always, among his associates, as "Long Ted". It may seem strange that the aristocratic Monson should invite a bookie's clerk for the shooting season, but doubtless he had his reasons.

At any rate, Edward Sweeney or Davis left London and travelled to Scotland to meet Monson in Glasgow. It was then that he was rechristened Edward Scott and was suddenly transformed from a bookie's clerk into a consulting engineer. They travelled in the same steamer from Prince's Pier, Greenock, to the Kyles of Bute. But, once aboard the steamer, Monson didn't seem to know his old racing pal and they went their separate ways. On board Monson met the Paisley shipbuilder, a Mr. Donald, from whom he had arranged to buy the steam yacht, *Alert,* for £1200. They had an affable discussion.

Monson and Scott (as we must now call "Long Ted") travelled to Ardlamont on 8 August. Miss Edith Hiron, governess to the Monson children, thought Scott an odd fish when they met at dinner that night. Unlike the other men, he wore ordinary clothes instead of a dinner jacket, and she noticed that he dropped his "h's".

Next day Scott, the marine engineer, might have been expected to have a look at the *Alert.* Instead, he went out with Monson in the morning and had a bathe in Ardlamont Bay. After lunch Monson and Scott asked McNicol, the Ardlamont Estate joiner, for the loan of his small boat for two nights. McNicol agreed and Monson and Scott rowed it round from Ardlamont Ferry into Ardlamont Bay.

This was an odd thing to do, because Monson had already

hired a rowing boat from McKellar, the Tighnabruaich boat-hirer, and Cecil Hambrough had been using it regularly for fishing expeditions. There had been no complaints about McKellar's boat, but Monson told McNicol that it was "not extra safe". An even odder thing was that, in the afternoon, Monson and Scott took Monson's children out for a row in the boat which was "not extra safe". At that time Cecil Hambrough and Mrs. Monson were having a walk to Ard-lamont Point.

Now there was a difference between McKellar's boat, which they'd been using all the time at Ardlamont, and McNicol's, which they had just hired that day. McNicol's boat had a plug-hole, closed by a cork, in it. The regular boat had no plug-hole. Maybe this worried that great nautical engineer, "Long Ted", because after Monson had taken his children back to the house from their afternoon voyage, Scott was observed working with a knife in the boat without the plug-hole.

That night someone suggested at dinner that they should go splash-net fishing. Monson and Cecil changed into suitable gear, got the nets and went into one of the boats. Scott decided to stay on shore and watch the fun.

Now you'll recall that Monson and Scott had borrowed the McNicol boat because, according to Monson, it was safer than the McKellar boat. So maybe you'll be a bit surprised to know that Monson and young Hambrough went out in the McKellar boat, and the newly hired McNicol boat was left on the shore beside Scott. And I should add, just by the way, that Monson could swim and Cecil Hambrough could not.

What happened then is very difficult to say. Apparently they rowed some distance out, when the boat sank. Both Monson and Hambrough got ashore, soaked but safe! This is Monson's version – "Hambrough took off his coat and rowed, while I busied myself preparing the nets. While occupied with the nets, suddenly there was a bump, and the boat tilted and I fell over the side. At the same time the boat capsized, and for a minute or two I was entangled in the nets. Immediately on getting clear I called out for Hambrough, and then saw him sitting on the rock laughing. Hambrough, I knew, could not swim, so I told him to wait while I swam ashore and fetched another boat which was there."

But two things puzzled the police when they investigated this story. The first was that no local fishermen knew of any rocks in Ardlamont Bay. And the second was that a plug-hole had been cut in the McNicol boat, which had been innocent of a plug-hole that morning. No cork could be found for this plug-hole.

At any rate, after their soaking, Monson and Cecil went back to Ardlamont House with Scott, changed once again, and had a celebratory party. After all, they had escaped from the horrors of the deep. So they drank whisky until about one o'clock in the morning and, obviously in the mood for more enjoyable excitement, arranged to go shooting about five hours later. They got to bed, and were out at the entrance to the woods at 6.30 a.m.

We know what happened then. Monson, Cecil Hambrough and Scott entered the woods. Only Monson and Scott came out alive. They said that Cecil Hambrough had accidentally shot himself with his sporting gun while he was negotiating a dyke.

When the police discovered the story of the boating "accident", they charged Alfred John Monson and Edward Scott with attempted murder in Ardlamont Bay, and then with actual murder in Ardlamont Woods. They maintained that Scott had cut the hole in the boat, that this hole had been hidden by the fishing nets which Monson was "preparing", and that the idea was to drown the non-swimmer, Cecil Hambrough, while that fishy customer, A. J. Monson, swam ashore.

But, the police went on, the boat filled up too soon, and it sank so near the shore that Hambrough was able to get back to dry land without swimming. Disappointed in their endeavours, Monson and Scott took Hambrough into the woods next morning and shot him. Everyone believed it was an accident, and two days later Monson claimed the £20,000 insurance.

That was all very well, but the police were facing one formidable snag – Scott had disappeared! On the very afternoon of the shooting, he'd been seen waiting on Tighnabruaich Pier for the afternoon steamer back to Glasgow. And that was the last that was seen of "Long Ted"

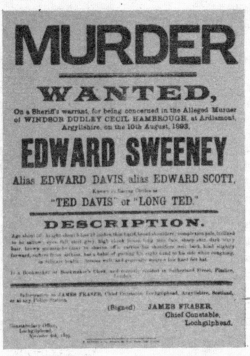

The bill circulated by the police

until long after the trial for murder of Alfred John Monson was over. When the police brought the charges of attempted murder and murder against Monson, they brought them against Scott too. But they couldn't find Scott and put out a "Wanted for Murder" bill which was circulated to police stations all over Britain. It ran –

MURDER

WANTED,

On a Sheriff's warrant, for being concerned in the Alleged Murder of WINDSOR DUDLEY CECIL HAMBROUGH, at Ardlamont, Argyllshire, on the 10th August, 1893,

EDWARD SWEENEY
Alias EDWARD DAVIS, alias EDWARD SCOTT,
Known in Racing Circles as
"TED DAVIS" or "LONG TED"

———————

DESCRIPTION.

Age about 30; height about 5 feet, 10 inches, thin build, broad shoulders; complexion pale, inclined to be sallow; eyes full, steel grey, high cheek bones, long thin face, sharp chin, dark wavy hair, brown moustache (may be shaved off), carries his shoulders well back, head slightly forward, suffers from asthma, has a habit of putting his right hand to his side when coughing, in delicate health; dresses well, and generally wears a low, hard felt hat. Is a Bookmaker or Bookmaker's Clerk, and recently resided in Sutherland Street, Pimlico, London.

———————

Information to JAMES FRASER, Chief Constable, Lochgilphead, Argyllshire, Scotland, or to any Police Station.

(Signed) JAMES FRASER,
Chief Constable,
Lochgilphead.

As we might say in Scotland, whaur's yer identikit noo? This exhaustive statement of the appearance and habits of Edward Sweeney may well have had its origin in London police observation, for "Long Ted" was not unknown to the Metropolitan constabulary. But it didn't seem to work. The Chief Constable of Argyll followed it up with an offer of a £200 reward for information leading to his recovery, but no one claimed it. The Argyllshire police traced Long Ted to London and interviewed the Sweeney family, but all they could say was that they thought their wandering boy had gone off to Australia.

A. J. Monson said after his trial that Scott had been in the North British Hotel in Glasgow all the time! But we know by now how much reliance could be placed on Monson's word.

At any rate, Monson went to jail to await his trial, while the police searched unavailingly for Scott. Eventually, on 12 December 1893, Monson appeared at the High Court in Edinburgh on charges of the attempted murder and murder of Cecil Hambrough. As Scott did not appear in answer to the charges, he was, to use the old Scottish phrase, "put to the horn", in other words he was proclaimed an outlaw.

It's just possible that Monson was delighted at Scott's disappearance because he might have turned out a rather awkward character. It's true that, being charged with murder, he could not appear as a witness. But he would have been asked to make a statement, and that might not have suited Monson's book at all. As it was, Alfred John Monson seemed to await his trial for murder with perfect equanimity. He received his lawyers and counsel graciously, he joked with his warders, and he always had his meals and his wine brought into his cell from a reputable restaurant outside the prison walls – paid for with money supplied by "Tot". Whatever you may think of A. J. Monson, he was not without a certain panache.

3

A trial invitation to tea

No murder trial in Scotland has ever had such a press as the Ardlamont Mystery. The trial of Alfred John Monson for attempting to murder Cecil Hambrough by drowning, and actually murdering him by shooting in Ardlamont woods on 10 August 1893, lasted for ten days and during that time more than 2,258,000 words on the case were printed by Scottish and English newspapers. One Edinburgh paper alone printed 52,000 words of description and 346,000 words of evidence.

The average Scottish newspaper was printing up to twenty full-size columns a day on the trial. In order to cover the case there were seventy reporters, twenty-one descriptive writers and fifteen artists in the High Court of Justiciary in Edinburgh. One of these artists (photography was not allowed in the High Court) was a woman – Miss Mary Cameron RSW. She was known to her colleagues as "Bloody Mary" because she was so keen on travelling to Spain to draw pictures of bull fights.

She represented that famous Scottish newspaper, the Oban Times (in whose territory the affair had taken place), and it was run by the Cameron family, who were also famous for their manufacture of pen nibs. Readers of my age may recollect the advertisement you saw in practically every railway station in Britain –

> *"They come as a boon and a blessing to men,*
> *The Pickwick, the Owl and the Waverley Pen."*

Indeed, Miss Cameron's sister, Mrs. Macauley, became Editor of the Oban Times and when she was semi-retired she was still in charge in the post of Consulting Editor. She was an indomitable woman who refused to recognise that in old age her eyes were growing weaker and would wear spectacles only in private. When the proof pages of her newspaper were put before her and she found difficulty in reading them, she immediately ordered a larger size of type to be bought and used. The result was that the Oban Times had the reputation of being the most easily read newspaper in Britain.

Miss Mary Cameron took after her sister. She was indomitable too, as she had to be in a profession where women were almost unknown. As the only woman among the Press representatives in the High Court of Edinburgh, Miss Cameron was quite conspicuous, especially as her fourteen fellow artists, all male, insisted with great gallantry that she should have a place right in front of them. Every morning of the trial, when the trap-door in front of the dock was opened, and the slim, well-dressed figure of A. J. Monson emerged, Mary would get her pencil and paper ready.

Invariably the accused, once he had settled himself in the dock, would look over towards her, smile, and give her a little bow. One of her Oban Times drawings of the Monson Trial shows the Judge, Counsel, the jury, the busy reporters and the accused sitting in the dock between two policemen. He is looking straight at the artist. Miss Cameron must have been pleased at this example of her work because she signed it – for whom is not known.

When Monson bowed to her each morning, Miss Cameron couldn't help bowing back but, in the middle of the murder

Faces in court. Beresford Loftus Tottenham is first from the right in the top row.

trial, the accused sent her a note, asking her to take tea with him in his cell during the afternoon adjournment that day. Miss Cameron felt, however, that Mr. Monson was far too forward, because they had never been introduced. She refused his invitation and after that stopped returning his morning bow.

I wonder what Mrs. Monson thought of this little charade each day? She sat at the back of the court, heavily veiled, and would speak to no one. She heard the character of her husband torn to shreds, as the Crown produced evidence to show that this man who was living in luxury at Ardlamont House was an undischarged bankrupt, that he had paid neither the £450 for the shooting which he had taken, nor £1200 for the yacht he had "bought". Even the very cartridge which killed Cecil Hambrough had not been paid for.

And here, in connection with the actual shooting in Ardlamont woods, the police brought in some interesting evidence. Cecil Hambrough usually shot with a 20-bore gun, "a boy's weapon", it was called. Monson used a 12-bore gun. Monson also used occasionally amberite "smokeless" cartridges, which could be fired from the 12-bore but not the 20-bore. On the morning of the "accident" Monson went to the Ardlamont gamekeeper and got the 20-bore gun, saying that Cecil wanted it.

As far as anyone knows, Hambrough carried this 20-bore gun into the woods, and Monson had the 12-bore. Three minutes after they entered the trees, the fatal shot was fired. After that, you have only Monson's word for what happened. All that can be said was that three men went into the woods and only two came out. They were Monson and his friend, Scott, who was merely holding a watching brief. They carried two guns, went straight to the house, removed the remaining cartridges from the two guns and cleaned the guns.

It was only after that that they raised the alarm and told the Ardlamont staff of the "accident". Monson's story, of course, was that, when they heard the shot, he and Scott went in the direction of the sound and found Cecil Hambrough already dead, having apparently killed himself with his own gun while climbing over a dyke. Cecil was notoriously careless with guns.

The police arrived and Monson took them to the body of Cecil Hambrough. Just near him the police found the wad of a 12-bore cartridge. The man in the street might readily assume that Hambrough had been shot by a 12-bore gun, and would recollect that the young man was carrying a 20-bore gun, and would therefore have his doubts about the "accident".

But in murder trials you frequently have "experts". The experts on either side in the Goatfell murder trial contradicted each other completely. The same thing happened here, although it's interesting to note that two of the doctors appearing for the prosecution, Henry Littlejohn and Patrick Heron Watson, had appeared for the defence in the Goatfell case. They were joined by a third expert, none other than the original of Sherlock Holmes. He was Dr. Joseph Bell, a famous figure in Edinburgh medical circles, and the man on whom Arthur Conan Doyle, a student of Bell's, based his world-known detective. Unfortunately, Dr. Bell did not get the opportunity of using his amazing powers of deduction in the Ardlamont case.

The three experts for the Crown said they thought Hambrough had been killed by a shot fired from nine feet behind him. They produced in court three trees which had stood in a line behind Hambrough's body. There was a rowan, a beech and a lime, and each was grooved by pellet marks made by the same shot.

The jury might have been interested to know that they were lucky in seeing these trees in court at all. When the police were investigating the case, they decided the trees might be needed in evidence, so they pitched a tent in the wood, and a policeman was set to guard the trees all night. On the first night the policeman was in the tent, he heard bushes rustle in the thick plantation about 2 a.m. He dashed out of the tent just in time to see a dark figure gripping the rowan tree. The policeman made for the figure but it disappeared into the undergrowth. Who could have wanted to destroy the rowan tree? And why?

This strange story was never mentioned in court, however. As far as the trees were concerned, the defence line was that the whole wood was full of pellets because it was such a favourite place for shooting. Dr. Henry Littlejohn, chief medical witness for the Crown, brought a demonstration skull with him, to show where the cartridge had entered Cecil Hambrough's head. Just as he had completed his evidence and was leaving the witness-box, Comrie Thomson, leading counsel for the defence, cried, "Stay, Dr. Littlejohn, stay!"

As Dr. Littlejohn paused, Comrie Thomson explained, "You have forgotten your head." Dr. Littlejohn seized the skull and said, "You are very right, sir. I can't afford to lose my head!"

Whatever might happen to Dr. Littlejohn's head, the fifteen good men and true of the jury had some difficulty in keeping theirs. They had all this contradictory evidence about the shooting. They had hour upon hour of evidence of the strange financial transactions in which Monson and his friends, Beresford Loftus Tottenham and Adolphus Frederick James Jerningham, and Major Dudley Hambrough (Cecil's father) and *his* friends were involved in.

Nevertheless, the Solicitor-General, Alexander Asher, put the whole matter plainly before them. It's difficult for us to judge now, because we know so much more than the jury knew, but it looked as if a verdict of Guilty against Monson was pretty certain. It was really two to one in Monson's favour, however. For the defence there was first of all the

Drama in court. Dr. Henry Littlejohn being cross-examined about his skull by Comrie Thomson for the defence.

spell-binder, Comrie Thomson, to dazzle the jury with eloquence rather than evidence, and second there was the judge, Lord MacDonald, to make confusion worse confounded.

Monson was lucky in having a judge who hated murder trials. Throughout the whole of his ten days' trial the accused looked calm and confident. He was ready to appreciate anything humorous or ludicrous in the evidence. And, of course, he gloried in being the centre of attraction. The court was packed every day, and crowds hung about the precincts hoping to get even a glimpse of Monson. Some of the officials thought they might let them have their wish. So, as long as the court was sitting, they would allow amateurs of crime to have a few seconds' look through a glass panelled door which gave a clear view of the dock. It was estimated that five hundred eyes looked at Monson every hour.

If Monson was conscious of this strange procession, he did not show any signs of resenting it. His man-of-the-world attitude faltered only once and that was when the Solicitor-General, in his address to the jury, described the attempt to drown young Hambrough on the night before he was shot dead. As Alexander Asher reconstructed the scene, making it clear that he considered that Monson and the outlawed Edward Scott had planned to kill Hambrough then, Monson grew pale. He leaned forward and spoke to his counsel, and Comrie Thomson asked Lord Macdonald for permission to allow the accused to go below to his cell for a few moments.

The trap-door in front of the dock was opened and down went Monson. After a few minutes he reappeared, looking as unmoved as ever and listened as the Solicitor-General addressed the jury and asked for a verdict of Guilty.

It was the turn of the defence. Comrie Thomson was not a great advocate, but he had a masterly manner with juries. He started his speech by going right back to the trial of

Madeleine Smith in that very court.

"Gentlemen," he said, "I remember more than five-and-thirty years ago sitting in one of these benches and hearing an advocate, who afterwards became a great judge, standing where I now stand, pleading for a woman who was sitting in that dock charged with the crime of murder. He opened his address to the jury in words which have since become historical, but I repeat them to you now because of their great truth and wonderful simplicity."

Comrie Thomson was described by one of his contemporaries as "silver-haired and golden-voiced". He leaned forward and fixed the jury with his glittering eyes as he repeated the words from the Madeleine Smith case – "Gentlemen, the charge against the prisoner is murder, and the punishment of murder is death; and that simple statement is sufficient to suggest to you the awful nature of the occasion which brings you and me face to face."

The jury had listened to more than eight days of confusing evidence. Comrie Thomson saw to it that the confusion was not made any less by his speech. You can pick holes in it when you read it today, but it must have sounded very impressive on 22 December 1893, in the High Court of Edinburgh.

"Gentlemen, we are all liable to make mistakes," he concluded. "I pray you make no mistake in this terribly serious matter. The result of your verdict is final, irreparable. What would any of you think if some day, it may be soon, this mystery is entirely unravelled, and it is demonstrated that that man is innocent, while your verdict has sent him to his death? He will not go unpunished if he is guilty. There is One in whose hands he is, Who is Infallible and Omniscient. 'I will repay, vengeance is mine, saith the Lord.'"

The jury must have been worrying all the time about the mysterious Edward Scott, who had disappeared after the shooting of Cecil Hambrough, and had never been seen again. They were not helped by the judge, who in his summing up, seemed to lean backwards, metaphorically speaking, to avoid saying anything against Alfred John Monson.

Years later, in his reminiscences, Lord MacDonald wrote of the Ardlamont murder case and confessed, "I went through nine days of anxiety, such as I have never experienced before or since. So dominant was the anxiety that, morning after morning, I awoke long before my usual time, and lay in a dull perspiration, turning things over and over, endeavouring to weigh them and determine their weight in the balance.

"Never before had I gone through an experience the least like it, and I am well pleased that I have never had a similar experience since. It was all the more trying because I felt quite unable to form a determined opinion in my own mind. The way never seemed to me clear."

Well, if the judge was sweating, literally, on the top line, the accused was haudin' a calm seugh. Lord MacDonald finished his address, and the jury filed out to consider their verdict. It was a dramatic moment. Two newspapermen, sitting just behind the dock, watched Alfred John Monson at this terrific crisis in his life. Mr. Monson rose and stretched himself. Then he turned round to the two reporters and smiled broadly. "Why am I like a railway engine?" the accused asked them. The newspapermen goggled at him and said something incoherent. Monson pointed to the hard wooden bench of the dock and said, "Because I've got a tender behind!"

I believe Monson murdered poor young Cecil Hambrough, but I can't help admiring his amazing audacity. The jury were out for 73 minutes. When they came back, the foreman announced a verdict of Not Proven (a unanimous verdict, it was discovered later). Lord MacDonald told Monson he could go.

Monson stood up smiling, and was congratulated by the two

Lord MacDonald

junior counsel for the defence. But the man whose eloquence had saved him, Comrie Thomson, walked out of the court with not even one glance at his client.

In doing this he was acting exactly the same as the defender who had succeeded in the Madeleine Smith case, getting her off when she was obviously guilty. Some time later Comrie Thomson is on record as saying, "I don't know whether Monson killed Hambrough, but he nearly killed me."

Now usually a person who has been found Not Proven or even Not Guilty of murder disappears from the public view. Even Madeleine Smith followed this pattern. But that was not Monson's way.

4

Vengeance is mine

Alfred John Monson was an undoubtedly remarkable man. As far as Scotland was concerned, he stayed not upon the order of his going, but went at once. Mrs. Monson seemed to bury her doubts about her husband, or maybe admired the way he had got away with whatever he had done, and the Monsons got together and went to Scarborough, where they doubtless had a better welcome than they would have received in Ardlamont. There were unpaid Monson bills all over the Kyles of Bute. Ardlamont Estate had been advertised at a starting price of £85,000. The effect of Monson's trial was such that the Lamonts were lucky to sell the place for £70,000.

One of the strange sequels to the murder trial was that some people tried to shoot themselves in the way that Monson said Cecil had done and found that they couldn't. The medical experts on Monson's behalf at the trial were sure that it was possible, but in a pub in the south of England an argument arose about the shooting. A local gamekeeper, Henry Card, said that Cecil could have inflicted the wound himself. He held his gun behind his back with one hand and reached down with the other to pull the trigger. Apparently Card did not realise that his gun was loaded and blew the top of his head off.

Monson did not worry about such trivialities. He had a career to pursue. He went to London and suddenly a Mr. Morritt, known as a ventriloquist, mesmerist and magician, announced that he was privileged to present a series of lectures on the Ardlamont Mystery by none other than A. J. Monson, in the Prince's Hall, Piccadilly. A big audience turned up for the first performance, but after the conjuring part of the show was over, Mr. Morritt had to announce that Mr. Monson would not appear after all – in spite of the fact that he had apparently been engaged at £125 a week.

Then Madame Tussaud announced that she would exhibit a wax model of A. J. Monson, wearing the very clothes he wore on that fatal morning at Ardlamont and equipped with the very gun which caused the death of Cecil Hambrough.

At once A. J. Monson brought an action against Madame Tussaud to restrain her from putting his model on show, and complaining that, though the verdict in his case was Not Proven, it was being exhibited in the Chamber of Horrors. Then, when he discovered that his effigy was also appearing in Louis Tussaud's waxworks in Birmingham, he brought a libel action against Louis as well.

What had happened, as far as Tussaud's in London were concerned, was that Monson's old financial pal, Beresford Loftus Tottenham had visited Tussaud's on 3 January 1894, and offered the clothes and a gun, plus a sitting by Monson, to John Tussaud. The price was agreed at £100, with £50 on account. A day or two later Tottenham returned the £50 and said that Monson had changed his mind.

Tussaud's pointed out that, so far from being exhibited in the Chamber of Horrors, the model of Monson had the Archbishop of Canterbury and the Pope on his right, and Queen Victoria and the Prince and Princess of Wales on his left. That seemed indeed distinguished company for an undischarged bankrupt. But what Tussaud's apparently forgot to explain was that these models appeared together in what was called Napoleon Room No. 2, which included the entrance to the Chamber of Horrors and Monson's effigy stood just outside the door where you paid the extra fee to have your blood run cold.

The case against the Tussauds was fixed for a later date, but in the meantime A. J. Monson had seemingly acquired a new taste for litigation. Some of his furniture was in a storage warehouse owned by Tottenham. Possibly Tottenham felt he was due some money back from Monson, but at any rate he sold some of the Monson furniture without asking Monson's agreement. Monson promptly prosecuted his old friend for theft, and Tottenham was sentenced to three months' imprisonment.

Some people in Scotland remembered reading how Beresford Loftus Tottenham had been described by Comrie Thomson, when he was conducting Monson's defence in the Ardlamont case, as "rather a queer fish. I do not think he is the kind of man that you and I [he was referring to the jury] – quiet-going Scottish folk – are in the habit of meeting, or even I do not know that any of us desire to make his more intimate acquaintance." So we need not shed a tear for Tottenham, who must have already known the old adage about there being no honour among thieves.

Eventually Monson's case against the Tussauds was heard before the Lord Chief Justice and a special jury in London. Tottenham was brought from prison and entered the witness box in custody of a warder. He told how he and Monson went to Tussaud's in a cab. Monson had brought along a suit of clothes but had no gun, so they stopped in Bond Street and bought a gun. Monson stayed outside in the cab, while Tottenham saw John Tussaud and arranged the deal. When he returned to the cab and explained that they'd get £100, Monson said that the price was too low and that he wouldn't take it, so Tottenham returned the £50 he'd received in advance. It did not take long for the jury to reach their verdict.

They found for the plaintiff and awarded him one farthing damages and one shilling for the detention of his suit, and Monson had to pay all his own costs.

He did not lie low for long. A few weeks after the libel case it was announced that he was writing a book which would clear up the whole Ardlamont mystery. When Monson's book did appear it turned out to be a shilling pamphlet of 72 pages. It was entitled "The Ardlamont Mystery Solved, by Alfred J. Monson, to which is appended Scott's Diary".

The main part of Monson's book was an attack on Scottish criminal procedure. "If the accident to the late Cecil Hambrough had taken place in England," he wrote, "I should never have been accused of murdering him."

What interested the readers, though, was what Monson called Scott's Diary. The final entries were –

Dec. 12 to 22. Have been present in court every day. Ready, if wanted, but never had any doubt about result.
Dec. 25. A Merry Christmas.

This interested the mysterious Mr. Scott too. Although he had been declared an outlaw in the High Court of Edinburgh, he suddenly appeared in London and said that he'd never kept a diary in his life!

"The Ardlamont Mystery Solved by Alfred J. Monson" got a bad Press and was a complete flop. But shortly after it appeared a pale, weedy man asked for an interview with the Editor of the Pall Mall Gazette in London. To the Editor he explained that he was Edward Scott, the missing man in the Ardlamont case, that he couldn't stand the lies which Monson was telling about him and wanted to write the truth in the Pall Mall Gazette.

When the Editor was certain that this was really Scott, he got in touch with Scotland yard. He wanted Scott arrested in the Pall Mall Gazette office so as to give a really sensational start to the new series of articles. But Scotland Yard had

"Mr. Scott"

scored the name of Scott from their list of wanted men. They just weren't interested.

So now the Pall Mall Gazette published Scott's story. He said that, on the fateful day of the shooting, he had left Ardlamont "because neither Mr. Monson nor myself had anything to hide". Monson, however, had given him the name of Scott and pretended he was a ship's engineer, and "Long Ted" didn't want his real name of Sweeney to be revealed, nor the fact that he was a bookie's clerk.

In London he read that he was wanted for murder. "I am a moral coward; I must confess it," he wrote in the Pall Mall Gazette. "I must also lack much reasoning power in the hour of danger, for I had but one idea, and that was flight." So he shaved off his moustache, put on an old suit, labelled his bag "Mr. White", and fled.

But his reasoning power didn't do so badly when he discovered that Scotland Yard were no longer interested in him. He saw no reason why he should remain an outlaw in Scotland, because outlaws were not allowed to operate at Ayr, Hamilton, Lanark, Musselburgh, Perth and other such interesting places. (For the uninitiated, these are Scottish racecourses.)

And so Edward Sweeney (alias Scott), commission agent, 66 Meadow Road, Clapham, told the Lords Commissioners at Edinburgh on 4 May 1894, that he was now prepared to stand his trial, and asked that he should no longer be outlawed. When the case was called in Edinburgh on 21 May, no one appeared for the Crown. So Scott had no case to answer, and the three Law Lords on the Bench expressed their disapproval of the prosecution. They told Scott he was no longer an outlaw and no longer charged with murder.

Meanwhile Alfred John Monson was not idle. He made an appearance in Edinburgh too, but it was in a theatre instead of the courts.

In April, 1895, Mr. Morritt, mesmerist and magician, was billed to appear at the Operetta House, Edinburgh. One evening there was printed in an Edinburgh newspaper a letter from A. J. Monson saying, "I challenge Mr. Morritt to try his hand on me, with a view to clearing up the Ardlamont Mystery. I see that he is to appear at the Operetta House on Monday next, and as I shall be in Edinburgh at the same time, I am willing to afford him an opportunity of publicly testing his theories."

On 25 April, the very day on which the challenge was to be made in the Operetta House, William Roughead was walking along Princes Street. Suddenly he saw ahead of him the man whose fortunes he had followed during the ten days of the Ardlamont murder trial in the High Court of Edinburgh – Alfred John Monson himself.

Monson, in tall hat and perfect clothes, was walking with a man Roughead didn't know. They turned up Lothian Road and went into a pub. Roughead hadn't the courage to follow them, and he regretted that all the more bitterly when he went to the Operetta House that evening and saw that Monson's companion of the morning was none other than

Mr. Morritt, mesmerist and magician.

Mr. Morritt performed various tricks and then he came forward to the front of the stage and said, "If Mr. Monson is in the building, I shall have pleasure in accepting his challenge." Mr. Monson immediately rose in the Dress Circle, and the mesmerism was announced for nine o'clock the following night.

William Roughead went back to the Operetta House on the Tuesday evening and saw Mr. Morritt put Mr. Monson into a trance. Then the mesmerist asked the audience to suggest questions Mr. Monson might be asked.

"Did you murder Mr. Hambrough?" Monson was asked. In his trance he replied, "No." "How was Cecil Hambrough killed?" was the next question, and the mesmerised Monson replied, "I don't know." Somebody up in the gallery shouted, "Stick a pin in him!"

Roughead had got a seat in the side circle as close to the stage as possible and, when this shout came from the gallery, he saw the hypnotised man smile.

A Doubting Thomas asked if Mr. Monson had been paid for this appearance and Mr. Morritt replied that there was no agreement with Monson whatever. The gentleman had come forward voluntarily to prove his innocence of the alleged crime. Mr. Roughead, remembering Princes Street and the pub in Lothian Road, had his doubts.

I had thought that that ended Monson's association with Scotland but, when I wrote about this case in the Glasgow Evening News some years ago, I received a letter from a lady in Glasgow. It read:

"My parents were great friends of Mr. and Mrs. McLeod who had a waxwork on North Bridge in Edinburgh. I remember well Mrs. McLeod telling the story of her meeting with A. J. Monson of the Ardlamont case after he was a free man.

One day a man went past the pay-box and didn't offer to pay. Mrs. McLeod called, 'Pay here, please, before you go up.'

Still no notice was taken, so she ran upstairs after him and again said, 'Please pay at the desk.' He sharply turned on her and exclaimed, 'Pity a man has to pay to look at himself.'

She said, 'Who may you be?' He replied, 'Monson,' and going forward and never paying, he said in a very high-falutin' voice: 'Where have you got me?'

She led him to a small ante-room, where Monson and Hambrough were depicted in a moor scene, encased in glass, guns in hand, surrounded with heath and ferns, etc., and very well done.

Monson took a good look and exclaimed, 'By Jove, where did you get that suit? That's the one I was wearing!' Mrs. McLeod, disgusted by this time, turned to him and said, 'That's our secret.'

She said he was a smart scamp, full of his own importance, and almost rude.''

It must be said, however, that A. J. Monson had a better experience than his quondam friend, Edward Scott. Perhaps because he heard of Monson's stage appearances, Scott decided to emulate him a year later. He chose Glasgow, however, and a former conductor of the orchestra in the Gaiety Theatre, Sauchiehall Street, told me what happened.

When it was announced that Scott was going to appear at the Gaiety there was a packed house. My friend, in the conductor's seat, gave him a fanfare. The audience just sat and hissed, and not a word of Scott's story came across the footlights. At last, amid a storm of hissing, he walked off the stage. He did not appear in Scotland again.

Neither, as far as I can discover, did Alfred John Monson. He was involved in various strange cases in the South, including an unsuccessful attempt by Mrs. Monson to get the £20,000 insurance on the life of the murdered Cecil Hambrough. As Alfred John Wyvill he lived for a while near Douglas, Isle of Man, and when his house went on fire (a habit Monson's residences had), he claimed £500 insurance for jewellery. When it was found that his real name was Monson, he lost the claim.

He became a money-lender's tout in London and was involved in at least one attempted murder. He specialised in trapping young men who were heirs to estates, as Cecil Hambrough was. Like most "fly men", Monson was eventually caught. In 1898 he was charged along with two others with conspiring to defraud the Norwich Union Life Assurance Society. He was found guilty and sentenced to five years penal servitude. Monson had hardly got behind prison bars than he brought a suit for divorce against his wife. "It is alleged," said a London newspaper, "that Mrs. Monson was guilty of infidelity in the year 1891 with a person unknown, and later in that year with another person. The other person is both known and remembered; he is the late Cecil Hambrough. Since the death of the late Cecil Hambrough at Ardlamont, Monson has had two children by his wife."

Monson's divorce suit was thrown out, and Mrs. Monson, following the prevailing fashion, wrote a book. In it she told of the dreadful life she had lived with the arch-swindler Monson – although she didn't actually accuse him of the murder of Cecil Hambrough.

Poor young Cecil's parents, Major Dudley and Mrs. Hambrough, did not forget. For many years there appeared an In Memoriam notice in the Glasgow Herald on every 10 August. It read:

"In loving memory of our dear son, Windsor Dudley Cecil Hambrough, found shot dead in a wood at Ardlamont, Argyllshire, August 10th, 1893, in his 21st year. 'Vengeance is Mine, I will repay, saith the Lord.'"

THE PERFECT MURDER

The cottage. The window through which the gun was fired is marked with a cross.

1

The Beauty of Beith

The Firth of Clyde is remarkable for a great deal more than merely being the most beautiful estuary in the world. It's also remarkable for the fact that one side of it is Highland, while the other is Lowland Scotland. Even today there are strongly differentiated characteristics between the people of Dunoon, Rothesay and Arran, and those of Largs, Troon and Ayr. But murder is no respecter of places and it has flourished as much on the Lowland side as on the Highland.

I have already described the two great murder cases on the Highland side of the Firth – the Goatfell murder (if it was a murder) and the Ardlamont Mystery (if it was a mystery). Now we cross over to the Ayrshire coast for the perfect crime at Portencross, and the Lowland side can show as baffling a murder as was ever committed anywhere. To this day it remains unsolved, and I don't suppose that anyone will solve it now, though it happened in 1913. It's all very well to argue as to whether or not John Watson Laurie really did kill Edwin Robert Rose in the Gully of Springs on Glasgow Fair Monday, 1889, or whether or not Rose slipped and met his death accidentally. In the Ardlamont case there are plenty of people (like myself) who feel that the verdict of Not Proven was a farce, and that Alfred John Monson shot young Cecil Hambrough on that August morning.

But what do you do when there is a murder with no accused and, naturally, no trial, when there are several suspects but no motives, when the police admit that they are completely baffled, and even the newspapers, which usually have their solutions, give up the whole affair as a bad job? If any of my readers can throw any light whatever on the Portencross murder, I shall be delighted to hear from them.

Before we have the facts of the murder, let's examine the scene. It has changed considerably since 1913. Then Portencross was a point, a most picturesque point, on the Ayrshire coast between the bay of Largs and the bay of West Kilbride. There is a ruined castle on the Portencross promontory looking straight across to the island of the Wee Cumbrae, where there is a twin castle. They were two guard points watching for any invaders coming up the eastern shore of the Firth of Clyde. The way to Portencross by Largs and Fairlie was a rough shore track which skirted the grounds of Hunterston Castle and came to a high cliff with three peaks. These peaks are still known as the Three Sisters, and just below the cliff of the third, or most southerly peak, is a whitewashed farm cottage called Northbank.

Northbank Cottage is still there, but its surroundings are somewhat changed since 1913. The enormous Hunterston Nuclear Power Station has been built on the shore side of the Hunterston Estate. The whole character of the area has been altered, and it's difficult to think of Northbank as a very remote cottage indeed. In 1913 a farm road ran from Northbank to the shore and then followed the line of rocks along to a fairly narrow pass between high rocks. This road led into the clachan of Portencross, which consisted of the castle ruin, a pier, a boarding-house, a farm, a post office and one or two houses.

It's rather built up now, though tremendously popular during summer weekends because of its beautiful situation. The one road leads inward from Portencross, past the West

Kilbride golf course and with glimpses of Seamill to the south, and ascends to the town of West Kilbride. Portencross people treat West Kilbride as their metropolis, though the towns of Ardrossan and Saltcoats are really not so very much farther away.

All these places between Largs and Saltcoats are closely linked now, but in 1913 lack of communications made each town or village seem quite isolated. Portencross was considered then to be quite out of the world, and Northbank Cottage, a thousand yards away from the clachan of Portencross on one side, and nearly a mile from the farm of Fences on the other, was regarded as a most lonely place.

Three people came to live in Northbank Cottage during the month of May 1913. They were a retired farmer-baker-evangelist named Alexander MacLaren, his wife, and his sister-in-law, Miss Mary Speir Gunn. MacLaren was sixty, and his wife a year older, but Miss Gunn was a youthful

Alexander MacLaren and wife

Murdered! Mary Gunn, "the beauty of Beith".

49. She had been a beauty as a girl, and was still considered to be a remarkably handsome woman. They had travelled together to Portencross from a farm in Perthshire.

The night of Saturday, 18 October was a dark and stormy
one. The three occupants of Northbank Cottage had their tea,
and then they settled down round the fire in the parlour. Mrs.
MacLaren and Miss Gunn sat on either side of the fire and
knitted as they listened to Mr. MacLaren reading aloud. Mr.
MacLaren sat in an armchair facing the fire, with his back to
the one window of the room. He had an oil lamp on a table
beside him and, at Miss Gunn's request, he'd picked a book
by W. W. Jacobs, her favourite author, for the reading. It was a
happy, domestic, Saturday night scene.

Now and again one of the women would glance out at the
rain beating against the window pane. The blinds were not
drawn because they considered themselves so far away from
everybody else that there was no need to draw them.

The time was around 8.30 p.m., and Mr. MacLaren had reached a particularly funny bit of the W. W. Jacobs story. They all laughed and settled down again. Mr. MacLaren cleared his throat and took up the story once more.

And at that moment there was a shattering roar from the window. Mrs. MacLaren saw a flash and smoke, and then what looked like the muzzle of a rifle or revolver pointing through the smashed pane.

The book was shot from MacLaren's hands. Miss Gunn jumped up from her seat in alarm, and then a fusillade of shots rang out. Miss Gunn clutched at her breast and cried, "Oh, Alex, I'm shot!" and fell to the floor.

Mrs. MacLaren had risen on the other side of the fire, but her husband jumped towards her shouting, "Floor! Floor!", meaning that that was the safest place to be.

But two more shots were fired, and Mrs. MacLaren sank down beside her sister. It was only as he crouched on the floor that MacLaren realised that the first shot had hit the index finger of his left hand and shattered it to the bone.

He lay there and tried to comfort the two wounded women. But he could see that Miss Gunn was badly hurt. There were no more shots – only the howling of the wind and the rattling of the rain at the broken window.

MacLaren rose and stared wildly round the shambles that had, a moment before, been a peaceful family scene. Then he ran out of the house and round into the garden from which the shots had come. In the darkness he could see nothing. He then ran to an outhouse where he had a collie dog and an eight-month-old pup. They had given no warning barks to indicate that there was a stranger about the grounds.

He loosed the dogs and tried to search round the cottage. But it was hopeless and he set off, stumbling in the storm, for Portencross, more than half a mile away.

Alexander Murray, the farmer at Portencross, was upstairs in his bedroom when he heard somebody burst into the house. "Come down! Come down!" a hoarse voice shouted. "We are all shot!" Murray rushed out on to the landing and saw that it was MacLaren, white faced and wild eyed, who stood in the hall. The farmer's wife rushed out too and saw the blood on McLaren's hand. "What's wrong with your finger?" she asked.

MacLaren looked at her as though he would go mad. "I'm shot, my wife's shot, and Miss Gunn's shot!" he shouted hysterically, then suddenly wheeled about and ran out of the door into the darkness.

The farmer hurried to the Laird's house at Auchenames, nearby, and discovered that MacLaren had just been there, and that the Laird had 'phoned to West Kilbride for the police.

As Murray got back to the main road, he met a taxi with a doctor and two policemen in it, making for Northbank. The police and the doctor went into the parlour of Northbank and found Mrs. MacLaren standing in the middle of the room, holding on to a table. Blood was oozing out of her back on to her dress. Miss Gunn was lying, covered in blood, in front of the fire. The doctor found she was dead. She had been shot thrice and one of the bullets had struck her in the heart. The doctor put Mrs. MacLaren to bed. She had been wounded twice, and he extracted a bullet from her back.

The police turned their attention to Alexander MacLaren, who was babbling incoherently from shock. They didn't know whether or not to believe his story, so they took him to West Kilbride Police Station. He was closely questioned and stammered out his account of the affair. The police went back to Northbank Cottage to see if they could find any traces of the murderer. They went into the garden outside the bullet-shattered window. The rain was still pouring down but they managed to make out three pairs of footprints near the window. And just below the window they found a bullet.

2

Rumour runs wild

The police had brought Alexander MacLaren back to Northbank Cottage. He sat in the room where the murder had been committed, while they searched the house. They collected two pairs of boots and the boots which MacLaren was wearing and by torchlight compared them with the footprints in the garden. But the footprints had been almost washed away by the heavy rain and, as far as the police could make out, none of them fitted Alexander MacLaren's boots.

A policeman whose job was to search the cottage came back with a shotgun which seemed to have been recently fired. When MacLaren was asked to explain he said he had been out shooting rabbits that morning. He directed them to the kitchen and there was a dead rabbit lying on the kitchen table. The police then compared the bullet they had found in the garden and the bullet which Dr. More of West Kilbride had taken out of Mrs. MacLaren's back with MacLaren's shotgun, they could see that the gun could not have fired these bullets. Ballistic experts examined the bullets later and said they had been used in a heavy Army revolver of the Colt type.

MacLaren was allowed to go to bed and a policeman guarded the house all night. Next morning Mrs. MacLaren was well enough to be interviewed. She corroborated her husband's story and said that, though she had been shot, she never lost consciousness. She described how she and her sister had been sitting knitting as they listened to her husband reading a book by W. W. Jacobs. She had actually seen the flash of the first shot, and the muzzle of a rifle or a revolver at the broken window.

She fell to the floor but, after MacLaren ran out to get his dogs and search the grounds, she managed to rise. No one, she said, had entered the cottage until MacLaren came back with the doctor and the police.

This was rather a facer for the police, who had decided right away that this was an attempted robbery. But it was surely a queer hold-up man who shot at people through a window and then ran away. The average hold-up man would surely have entered the house, menaced his victims with his revolver, and made them hand over their money and valuables. The West Kilbride police, of course, were at a disadvantage. For one thing, incredible though it may seem, they had no telephone in the local police station in 1913. When MacLaren had run to Auchenames to tell the Laird about the shooting, the Laird had to 'phone a friend in West Kilbride to go and tell the police!

There had not been enough local police on the night of the murder to make any real search of the area. They did their best, but Northbank Cottage stood in front of an almost unscalable cliff. A few fields lay along a rock-bound coastline. There was then a rough track towards the village of Fairlie which the police considered would only be taken by a man who knew the district well.

There was, of course, the path into Portencross. But the shooting had occurred about 8.30 p.m., and it was fair to assume that anyone making off in the Portencross or West Kilbride direction could be seen. So the police put a basket over each of the footprints in the garden to protect the prints

The morning after. Inspector Grant, the Chief Constable of Ayr and MacLaren, with his arm in a sling, at the cottage.

until plaster casts could be made of them.

On Sunday, 19 October Chief Constable Robertson-Glasgow of the Ayrshire Constabulary arrived at Portencross with his leading detectives. In a district now wild with rumours it was said by the wiseacres that the chief would not be long in solving this strange murder. Why? Because he had been a District Inspector of the Royal Irish Constabulary and had considerable experience of "moonlighting" cases in Ireland, where firing through windows was apparently quite common.

But the Chief Constable soon realised that he was facing a baffling mystery. He had six bullets – two were found embedded in the arcmchair in which Alexander MacLaren had sat reading on that fateful Saturday night. And he had six footprints – four of which were so indistinct that they were practically valueless.

Bullets were not much good without the weapon which had fired them, and there was no trace of a Colt or any other type of revolver. Footprints were not much good without boots to fit them, and the boots which made the marks seemed very ordinary boots indeed.

A rumour got around the district that the footprints were of golf boots, and this was regarded as most significant, because the West Kilbride golf course was so near Portencross. But golfers, though irrational beings, have seldom resorted to murder.

The police said that the boots which made these prints could have been used for golf, but they could also have been used for any number of other pursuits.

One suggestion for the complete disappearance of the murderer was that, thinking he had killed the entire family, he had committed suicide by throwing himself into the sea at Portencross. The police were searching the rocks along the waterfront, as well as the Ardneil woods behind the Three Sisters.

One member of a foursome playing over the West Kilbride golf course took his eye off the ball long enough to discern what he thought was a black body being washed about among the rocks on the sea side of the links. The four golfers threw down their clubs and ran across the links to the rocks. But, as they reached the "body", it flipped its tail, dived off the rocks and swam away. It was a seal.

The suicide theory, of course, did not fit in with the robbery motive, and that was still the basis on which police investigations were proceeding.

Alexander MacLaren and his wife had kept themselves very much to themselves since arriving at Portencross in May, but the general idea in the district was that they were fairly well off. On the Thursday before the murder MacLaren had gone to a cattle sale in Perth, where he was disposing of the remaining sheep he had kept at his farm in Taynuilt. He came back with a cheque for something like £100, and it was possible that some undesirable characters thought he had brought the £100 back in cash.

But, on the Saturday night of the murder, all he had in the house was £15, together with about £20 in his own pockets. No one had attempted to rob him, nor had any thief entered Northbank Cottage after the shooting, when its only occupants were a dying woman and a wounded one. Though MacLaren himself said that he had no positive theory about the motive for the murder, he doubted that it was robbery. He said that his sister-in-law, the handsome Miss Gunn, had gone shopping in West Kilbride on the Saturday afternoon. He had gone out to meet her on the way back, and they met on the road between Portencross and West Kilbride.

About that time a stranger came along and passed the time of day with them, but MacLaren didn't pay any particular attention to him. They got back to Northbank Cottage, the cow was milked, and they all sat down to their tea. MacLaren scouted the theory that anybody in the district had a grudge against him.

Chief Constable Robertson-Glasgow, however, decided that enquiries should be made into the lives of the three people concerned in the Portencross murder before they arrived at Portencross at all. And what the police discovered about the murdered woman, Miss Mary Speir Gunn, led them to change their minds about the possible motive for the murder. They no longer thought that robbery was the motive. They now concentrated on the idea that the motive could have been revenge.

Police enquiries into the lives of Alexander MacLaren and his wife Jessie led them to believe that the MacLarens had led exemplary lives. Mrs. MacLaren was the eldest and Miss Gunn the youngest of three sisters, the daughters of Gilbert Gunn, famous as one of the strongest men in Scotland. Gilbert was a railway contractor at Gateside, Beith, and the favourite story that was told was how on one occasion he had carried for a wager a lade of meal, a cheese and a ham for nearly a mile.

Miss Mary Gunn became the first telephone operator in Beith around 1883. At that time Alexander MacLaren was manager of the Glengarnock Iron and Steel Company's store at Dalry. He married Mary Gunn's eldest sister Jessie, who was twelve years older than Mary. After living in Beith for a while, the MacLarens went off to Port William in Wigtownshire, where Alexander opened first a general store and then a bakery. Mary Gunn was transferred from Beith to the Ardrossan telephone exchange, but gave up her job as a 'phone operator when her brother-in-law asked her to come to Port William to help to run the business.

So Miss Gunn joined the MacLarens at Port William and did not leave them again for more than twenty years. She took over the bakery side of the business. Alexander MacLaren himself was interested in evangelism and education. He built an Ebenezer Hall for evangelistic meetings which he conducted himself and was also on the local school board.

A post office was included in the general store at Port William, and Mr. MacLaren decided to move when ge got the chance to take over the post office at Taynuilt in the Highlands. He and his wife went North and Miss Gunn stayed at Port William until she had settled all the MacLaren affairs, then joined them at Taynuilt. Next Alexander MacLaren gave up the post office and took up farming.

Around that time Miss Gunn was not at all happy, because she had no longer a shop to attend to. She was just one of two women concerned in running the domestic side of a farm. Her middle sister had married and had emigrated to Canada. She kept on inviting the "baby" of the family to join her and her husband. All of a sudden Miss Gunn decided to leave Taynuilt for Saskatchewan.

Mary Speirs Gunn was, as I have said, the beauty of Beith. But there are some beauties who, for no reason anyone can discover, are destined to remain unwed. She was still heart-whole when she went to Canada, but there in Saskatchewan she met a man who fell in love with her.

The MacLarens knew all about this love affair, for Miss Gunn was an ardent correspondent. But something went wrong with it for, after a little more than a year in Canada, Miss Gunn suddenly left the country and came back to stay with the MacLarens at Taynuilt. Shortly after that Alexander MacLaren sold his farm and retired, with his wife and his sister-in-law, to the peace of Portencross.

So now one theory that the police were working on was that the disappointed lover had come across from Canada to make Miss Gunn his own – or kill her. And after he had killed her, of course, he would naturally commit suicide, preferably by throwing himself into the sea off Portencross.

This was a very nice theory and it was canvassed in the newspapers for some considerable time. Then the police made enquiries in Saskatchewan and discovered not only that Miss Gunn's erstwhile lover was still alive, but that he was positively in Saskatchewan on the night of 18 October 1913!

And that disposed of one solution as to the identity of a mysterious, bearded stranger who was said to have been seen around West Kilbride and Portencross on the day of the murder. But the police were following up clues to strangers all over the place.

They surrounded a plantation near Portencross because a mysterious man had been seen in it. They got the man all right, but he was merely there to set snares for rabbits.

Then the police were told of a strange man who, at West Kilbride Station, had demanded a ticket for Largs and said he had no money. And this on the night of the murder. When they investigated this peremptory passenger they discovered that he was a Largs business man who wanted to get home from West Kilbride and *had* no money!

Then there was the theory that the murderer had escaped by boat from Portencross. On that dark and stormy night the only place he reasonably could have reached was the Wee Cumbrae island, just opposite Northbank Cottage. It was hardly the spot where a murderer would choose to conceal himself. Apart from that, there were only two boats at Portencross and neither was missing.

The Ayrshire police were criticised for not using bloodhounds in the search for the murderer. They had, in fact, taken along an Airedale terrier, "specially trained for the job", and had searched the whole shore, all the ground round Northbank and the top of the Three Sisters. They were very hampered by the long grass which grew everywhere and a great deal of time was spent in cutting it so that a better search could be made.

A fisher for Scottish pearls came along with a suggestion for examining the stretch of jagged rocks along the front at Portencross. The police had been covering this area with long poles, which they poked into pools and crevices in an endeavour to discover a body or a revolver or some clue. Now, acting on the pearl fisher's idea, they had a couple of wooden boxes with glass bottoms made. When the sea was calm enough, they went out in small boats and put the glass-bottomed boxes over the side. When such a box was eight or nine inches under water, the police were able to scan the very floor of the sea.

Where the floor of the sea was sand, they had a wonderful view. But among the rocks at Portencross there was a tremendous amount of seaweed, and most of the time the police could see nothing else but dark brown curling fronds which could have concealed almost any size of object from a revolver upwards.

Another theory that the police had to investigate was that the murder was the work of a maniac. Some three months before the murder, the whole of West Kilbride was in a ferment because a mentally deranged man was roaming about the houses at night. He would rush up to a door and ring the bell or else batter on the panels. He got into one villa through the kitchen window and had to be put out by a policeman. But it was proved that this unfortunate could have had nothing to do with the Portencross affair. And at length the police decided that, if the murder was the work of a maniac, he must have been sane enough to commit the perfect crime that we occasionally read about in crime thrillers. For the Portencross murder was nothing short of that. The murderer had left no trace or clue. As far as the police and the public knew, there wasn't even a motive for the murder.

And then, all of a sudden, the Ayrshire police transferred their attention to Glasgow. Everyone in West Kilbride began to breathe again. Glaswegians, as we all know, are capable of any sort of crime. "Sensational developments are hourly expected," said one newspaper. "Arrest imminent in Portencross Case," said another.

3

Suspects and slander

Very little work was done in West Kilbride on the day that the Ayrshire police went to Glasgow. In the early evening the inhabitants, except those who lived in the villas, congregated in small groups in the town and waited anxiously for the "sensational" news which had been promised by the newspapers. Doubtless the inhabitants of the villas were just as interested as *hoi polloi,* but they weren't going to show it.

All of a sudden two struggling men were seen being conveyed to the West Kilbride Police Station. The watching groups coagulated into a big crowd outside the Station. They were sure that this was the long expected arrest at last. But, in the words of a newspaper of the time, the two men were "ordinary, innocent drunks".

The police would say nothing whatever about their famous visit to Glasgow. But it soon became obvious that they had drawn a blank there too. They kept on searching the rocky shore at Portencross, and the ground round Northbank Cottage, and the Ardneil wood on the cliff behind the cottage. But they found no more than they'd found on the night of the murder – six bullets and six footprints.

Meanwhile, an enterprising Glasgow printer had published a picture postcard entitled "Portencross Murder. Scene of the Crime". It was a view of the MacLarens' cottage and possessed no particular artistic merit, but it sold in thousands.

A month after the murder had been committed, Chief Constable Robertson-Glasgow, of the Ayrshire Constabulary, put out a poster from his office.

"£100 Reward," read the poster, "will be paid to the person or persons (not being the actual perpetrator) who give such information as will lead to the apprehension and conviction of the party who committed the shooting outrage at Portencross, West Kilbride, on Saturday, 18th October, 1913, by which Miss Mary Speir Gunn was fatally shot and Mr. and Mrs. Alex MacLaren injured. Information to be addressed to the Chief Constable of Ayrshire."

But nobody seemed to want the £100. Not another iota of real evidence came to the police.

Poor Miss Gunn, the faded beauty of Beith, was buried in the Southern Necropolis in Glasgow, with the plaid she was in the habit of wearing. Mrs. MacLaren, who had been shot in the back, was taken to Kilmarnock Infirmary. She was kept there until January 1914, when she was well enough to be conveyed by her husband to a friend's house in Dalry, not far from Beith.

Alexander MacLaren, a stocky, bearded man in a knickerbocker suit, gave quite a few interviews and voiced some dark suspicions. On one occasion there was a scene on the little bus which gave a shuttle service between West Kilbride and Portencross, when he accused a young local man, a student at Glasgow University, of traducing him.

But gradually the interest in the Portencross murder subsided, even in West Kilbride. In spite of the glorious summer many people were worried about what was happening in Europe. Even at home all was not well with the world. On a single day in Glasgow there were two murders, and a member of the Glasgow Stock Exchange who had been "hammered" that morning went up a close off St Vincent Street and committed suicide by cutting his throat with a penknife.

Everywhere the Suffragettes were demonstrating, sometimes rioting and burning. These were the Good Old Days, the end of that peaceful régime (so the greybeards told us) which vanished on 4 August 1914.

Mass murder took the place of individual killings and the Portencross murder was soon forgotten – except at Portencross and in Kilmarnock Sheriff Court. For there, a year and a month after the murder, a slander action was brought against Alexander MacLaren.

The action, demanding £1000 in damages, was brought by Mrs. Elizabeth Walker or Gibson, boarding-house keeper of Portencross Boarding-House – one of the few buildings in the wee clachan some thousand yards from the scene of the murder.

On 4 December 1914, it was announced that the record had been closed in Kilmarnock Sheriff Court of an action at the instance of Mrs. Gibson, wife of Andrew Gibson, of 104 Renfrew Street, Glasgow, against Alexander MacLaren, sometime residing at Northbank, Portencross, and now at Garnock Street, Dalry, concluding for £1000 damages in respect of an alleged slander.

In the words of the official report, "The pursuer avers that the defender falsely and calumniously made statements to the effect that she had participated in or had guilty knowledge of the murder of the defender's sister-in-law, Miss Mary Gunn, at Portencross on October 18th last year.

"In consequence of the defendant's statements an estrangement has resulted between herself and her husband, and her business has suffered very seriously."

The details of this action were sent from Kilmarnock Sheriff Court to the Court of Session in Edinburgh, and it was expected that a jury trial would be fixed, and the whole story would come out.

The Law works slowly, as we know, and it was 19 March 1915, some seventeen months after the murder, before the slander case of Mrs. Gibson against Alexander McLaren came up in the Court of Session. The Lord Ordinary fixed a date for the trial.

And then up got Mr. W. D. Patrick, counsel for Mrs. Gibson, and told the Judge that his client wished to abandon her action against Mr. MacLaren. So she had to pay all the costs, and lost her hope of damages of £1000. It was an expensive affair for Mrs. Gibson.

What was behind the action? That, I'm afraid, we do not know. The newspapers of the day barely reported the bringing of the action, and not one of them reported its abandonment. Of course, the Great War was on!

It's tempting to speculate on whether the slander action had anything to do with the Ayrshire police's sudden visit to Glasgow, where Mr. Gibson was living, or not.

And, talking of speculation, I should like also to speculate on a possible solution to the Portencross murder. I have already said what I thought actually happened in the Corrie of Springs on Goatfell. Let us examine the situation at Northbank Cottage.

In my examination of the case I have given the description of the Portencross murder according to what Alexander MacLaren told the police, and which his wife later homologated. But what if MacLaren was lying when he had his several interviews with the police?

Sir Arthur Conan Doyle was first, of course, when in one of his cases Sherlock Holmes said that the most remarkable point in the mystery was the dog that did not bark in the night. That can be said just as forcibly in the Portencross case. Alexander MacLaren had a collie and a pup in an outhouse just behind Northbank Cottage. If there was an intruder moving about the cottage grounds, why did the dogs not give the alarm by barking? If, on the other hand, it was a well-known step they would stay silent.

But what motive could MacLaren have for committing

murder? Could it be what best-selling authors used to call the eternal triangle? He had married the eldest of the Gunn girls, and she was a year older than he was. Almost from the start of the marriage, the MacLarens had been joined by Mary, the youngest of the daughters of Gilbert Gunn. She went to Saskatchewan and apparently had a love affair of some kind there. But for some reason – possibly the call of home? – she returned from Canada and joined the MacLarens once again.

Mrs. MacLaren at sixty-one could have been showing signs of her age. We know that Mary Gunn, though now forty-nine, was still regarded as a good-looking woman. She hadn't been called the Beauty of Beith for nothing. And here was Alexander MacLaren in constant touch with both these ladies.

Now I am sure that the vast majority of evangelists are the purest of the pure, and you'll recollect that MacLaren was an evangelist. When the most famous of our modern evangelists, Billy Graham, was conducting his big campaign in Glasgow, I got into trouble for saying on a Scottish radio programme, "A Matter of Opinion", that I was doubtful about the efficacy of evangelism since so often that kind of campaign resulted in a rise in the illegitimate birth rate.

All hell was let loose upon me. I mean that literally. In the middle of the night my telephone would ring and a voice would say, "Are you the Jack House who wrote about Billy Graham?" I would say yes, whereupon the voice would say, "May you burn in hell!" and the Christian would ring off.

I was invited by a Professor of Glasgow University and various other Graham supporters to prove that what I said about a rise in the illegitimate birth rate after an evangelistic campaign was true. I succeeded in giving a group of authentic statistics, but this did not satisfy my critics. I remained in the dog house.

A year after the Billy Graham campaign was over, I had as a features writer for the Glasgow Evening News to investigate the medical records for the previous twelve months. The illegitimate birth rate for the period did not come into the scope of my investigations, but I couldn't resist asking the official in charge of the medical records to have a look at the illegitimate birth rate nine months or so after Billy Graham. He found them without any difficulty. They were up!

However I did not rush into print and say, "See – I was right!" Indeed, this is the first time I ever revealed the rise in print. I did mention it to a Scottish psychologist who said, "Well, what do you expect if you're preaching 'Love, love, love' to impressionable teenagers?"

Now, it may be that evangelist Alexander MacLaren was preaching "Love, love, love" at his regular meetings in the Ebenezer Hall, and it's possible that the message eventually got to him. What if he began to prefer the comparatively young Mary Gunn to his elderly wife? One incident which has always struck me as unusual was that on the Saturday afternoon of the murder Miss Gunn had been shopping in West Kilbride and Alexander MacLaren had trudged up the steep road to meet her. Was it to carry her message bag, or did he want to make sure she was safe? Or was it an assignation for a special reason? Again, I am merely speculating.

But suppose that MacLaren had decided that he preferred the attractions of his sister-in-law to those of his wife and was so besotted that he had decided to remove his wife from the scene? He was a good shot but he would realise that, if he shot his wife with his own gun, the police investigators would soon prove that it had done the deed. So, on his frequent absences from Portencross around that time, he could have come into possession of an Army revolver with the appropriate bullets.

And so, that night, the three of them are sitting round the fire in the parlour, the two women knitting and MacLaren reading to them a story by W. W. Jacobs. When he judges the time is right, MacLaren stops reading, makes an excuse, and leaves the room. He collects the already loaded revolver, and goes out by the back door. The dogs, hearing their master's steps, make no noise.

MacLaren goes through the wind and the rain to the front of the cottage. It's possible that he has never fired a heavy revolver before and it's likely that he is very excited. He breaks the window with the muzzle of the revolver and starts firing. The revolver has a life of its own and he can't control his shots. He fires five and then, having worked out his alibi, he fires the last shot at his hand. That would account for the lone bullet lying in the garden under the window, and MacLaren considers that his wound will be proof to the police that he was in the room when the shots were fired through the window.

Now he runs across the few yards from the cottage to the rocks on the shore and throws the revolver into the water. He runs back to his home, looses the dogs, and enters the parlour to find that he has shot the wrong woman. Mary Gunn is dying and his wife is lying injured. This must have been the last straw to the already unstable man and could account for his actions when he ran to Portencross to raise the alarm.

All this, as I have said, is speculation and you may well ask the one big question – Why, if my theory is correct, did Mrs. MacLaren tell the police the same story that her husband had told them? It could be, the incident was so sudden and so shocking, that she might not remember whether her husband was still in the room or not. Shock has been known to cause amnesia. Or could she (and I admit that this seems rather far-fetched), having realised that her rival was dead, have decided not to say anything that would incriminate her husband? This, of course, begs the question – did Mrs. MacLaren know that her sister was her rival in her husband's affections?

I don't suppose we'll ever know.

THE MAN WHO
KILLED HIS MOTHER

John Donald Merrett as a boy

1

The earnest student

William Roughead was a great criminologist, a man learned in the law, and a perceptive and witty writer. But, having studied his works for many years, I have come to the conclusion that he had an Achilles heel. He was inclined to have the opinion that, if someone was accused of murder, that person was guilty. This is not uncommon, of course. My wife served on a jury concerned with a Glasgow gang murder and, when they retired to consider their verdict, one member of the jury opened the discussion by saying, "Well, he's in the dock, so he must be guilty."

I'm not suggesting that Roughead was as stupid as that – anything but. However, he seemed constantly to take the line of the Crown against the accused. He was right in the case of John Donald Merrett, tried at the High Court in Edinburgh in February 1927 for the murder of his mother in their flat in one of the most "refained" parts of the Scottish capital. William Roughead attended the trial and, on the last day of the hearing, the jury brought in a verdict of Not Proven. Later he was asked what he thought of it. He shook his head and said prophetically, "More will be heard of this young man."

How right Roughead was! John Donald Merrett not only murdered his mother but, in the fullness of time, killed twice again. Tom Tullett, a crime expert on a national newspaper, wrote a book about Merrett and entitled it *Portrait of a Bad Man*. Here are the facts, and you can judge for yourself.

John Donald Merrett was born in August 1908, and was the only issue of a Mr. Merrett and his wife, Bertha Milner. They lived in Southport. But Mr. Merrett was an engineer and he was asked, at a high fee, to go to Russia and supervise engineering works there. He took his wife and son with him. Mrs. Merrett did not like life in Russia, and it appears that Mr. Merrett did not particularly like his wife. She had a private income and decided to take young John to Switzerland. The idea was that, after a long holiday in Switzerland, she would rejoin her husband in Russia. But on 4 August 1914, the Great War started and Mrs. Merrett lost touch with her husband. She assumed that he had deserted her because it would have been comparatively simple, at the beginning of the war, for him to have joined his wife and son in Switzerland. In fact, she never saw her husband again. At the time of her death, he was reported to be somewhere in India, but he made no attempt to contact his wife's family.

When the German armies started to overrun Belgium and France, Mrs. Merrett decided to get as far away from Europe as she could. She chose New Zealand and lived there until 1924. Her son Donald (for some reason he was never known as John) went to school in New Zealand and proved himself a bright boy, though sometimes he was rather obstreperous. Mrs. Merrett thought it might be good for him to complete his education in England. He was now sixteen and she had a mind that he could be a credit to her in the diplomatic service. She thought of entering him for Oxford University.

They sailed from New Zealand back to Britain and Donald was sent to Malvern College while his mother made up her mind about a university for him. She found herself somewhat concerned about the post-war situation in such places as London and Oxford. The Great War had been over for nearly six years but the atmosphere of the country seemed still to be warlike – except that the enemy was no longer foreign. The newspapers were full of stories of strikes and crimes and also of the revolt of the young against what they thought was Edwardian (or even Victorian) stuffiness. What Mrs. Merrett heard of Oxford University did not appeal to her. She was worried about the possible effect of such an atmosphere on the apple of her eye, young Donald.

And so she thought of other options. She decided that she did not want Donald to go to a university where he would live apart from her. She thought of a place of learning where he could live with her at home and be under her eye. Someone recommended to her the University of Edinburgh. She went to see the city and the University and felt it was the answer. At first the city delighted her, the University had a high reputation and, if she found a suitable residence, Donald would live with her there. It should be said that she changed her mind about Edinburgh and described the capital in uncomplimentary phrases, but that was maybe not Edinburgh's fault.

Mrs. Merrett was 55. A friend of hers said, "Everything she did, she did to perfection." In March 1926, Mrs. Merrett rented a furnished flat at 31 Buckingham Terrace, Edinburgh, for four months. It was considered among one of the good New Town addresses. Donald was entered at the University as a student in the Faculty of Arts. Every morning after breakfast he collected his books and left the house, ostensibly for the University. In the evening he would usually come home, have a meal, and then retire to his bedroom. It was next-door to the sitting-room and was on the terrace front of the building, while Mrs. Merrett's was at the back.

Usually Donald locked his bedroom door because, he said, he didn't want to be interrupted in his studies. Also he complained of sleep-walking and Mrs. Merrett was afraid of his roaming about the flat in his sleep, and even more of his

Mrs. Bertha Merrett

somehow falling out of his bedroom window from the first floor to the terrace below. It was decided that a rope should be tied across the window to prevent Donald's possible disappearance. For her part, Mrs. Merrett was delighted that Donald was so studious, but sometimes in the morning he looked so tired and worn out that she was afraid that he was overworking. When she mentioned this to him, he shook his head and said that he was determined to carry on.

And that is what Donald undoubtedly did. He attended his classes at the University for only six weeks, then never went back. He had discovered the delights of the Dunedin Palais de Danse in Picardy Place and spent a lot of his time there and in similar pursuits. His special pursuit was named Betty Christie. She was a good-looking dance instructress and professional partner at the Palais de Danse. A visitor to the Palais without a partner could hire one for a regular fee for a stated time. But the Dunedin also had a system called "booking out". For fifteen shillings Donald could "book out" Betty for the whole afternoon, and for thirty shillings he could have her for the night.

How did he manage to get out of the flat without his mother knowing? It was quite simple. If she had gone out, there was no difficulty in leaving by the front door. But if she was still in the flat, the rope to keep him falling out of the window of his bedroom when he was sleep-walking did the trick. Donald simply untied it, attached one end to his bed, and lowered it over the window down into Buckingham Terrace. He also lowered the rope if he was going out by the front door because he had to have a climbing route back to his bedroom.

He had to be careful, of course, in his rope trick to make sure there was no one about in the street to see him. But in those March days of 1926 it was dark or getting dark by the time that Donald decided that he should make his rendezvous with Betty at the Dunedin Palais de Danse. It was

The house in Buckingham Terrace. Merrett's bedroom had the single window with balcony.

just as simple getting back to his room late at night. Since Buckingham Terrace was a most respectable place there was seldom anyone about after the time of walking of dogs. All Donald had to do was to make sure the coast was clear and then go back up the rope. There was also a convenient rone pipe which went from street level up the side of the building a foot or so from his bedroom window. Donald didn't worry anyway. The exercise was good for him and, besides, he'd have done anything to have a night out with Betty.

His other special friend at the Dunedin was a male dancing partner named George Scott, who sometimes joined Donald and Betty in their various ploys. Donald could "book out" George as well if it was necessary for any adventure the trio might think of undertaking. And you may consider that all this was quite remarkable in view of the fact that Mrs. Merrett allowed her son just ten shillings a week pocket money. Not only that, but he had to keep an account of his expenditure and show the notebook to his mother at the end of every week.

Strange to say, his expenditure book did not include the frequent "booking out" of Betty Christie from the Dunedin Palais de Danse, nor the price of two rings, one jade and one opal, for Betty, nor the cost of a motor-bike and later a motor racing cycle with sidecar. And it did not include the price of an automatic pistol and fifty cartridges. To coincide with all this extra expenditure Donald was assiduously practising the copy of his mother's signature. To do this he had torn the fly-leaf out of Mrs. Merrett's prayer book. He occupied some of the time in his locked bedroom tracing the signature on it through carbon paper on to plain paper, then going over it carefully with his pen.

On the morning of 13 March Mrs. Merrett was surprised to get a letter from the Clydesdale Bank saying that her account was in danger of being overdrawn and recommending that she should transfer some funds from her main account in

London. She decided to look into this odd circumstance later. But on 16 March she received another letter from the Clydesdale Bank saying that her account was now overdrawn.

And so, on the morning of 17 March, Mrs. Merrett felt inclined to talk to her son about these strange changes in her Edinburgh bank account. Apparently she didn't raise the subject at breakfast-time. Mrs. Merrett had a daily servant, Mrs. Henrietta Sutherland, who came in at 9 a.m. and worked until noon. That morning Henrietta arrived on time as usual, and Mrs. Merrett opened the door to her. She told Henrietta that breakfast was over, so they both went through to the sitting room and cleared the table there. Henrietta took the breakfast dishes into the kitchen and washed them. About a quarter to ten she decided to go into the sitting room and ask Mrs. Merrett what her next task should be. When she entered the room she saw Mrs. Merrett sitting at the table and busy writing. Donald was in an armchair in a recess on the other side of the room, reading a book.

Henrietta went back to the kitchen to make up the fire. Edinburgh was a cold place in March. All of a sudden she heard what she thought was a shot, followed immediately by a woman's scream, and the sound of a falling body. It was all so horrible that she didn't know what to do. While she was still trying to make up her mind to go back into the sitting room, Donald Merrett came into the kitchen, looking, she said later, as if he was going to cry. He blurted, "Rita, my mother's shot herself." He added that he had been "wasting" his mother's money and she had "quarrelled him" about it.

Henrietta went into the sitting room, followed by Donald, and saw Mrs. Merrett lying on the floor between the oval table and a bureau. She was bleeding from a wound in her right ear. Henrietta also saw that there was a pistol lying on the top of the bureau.

Now you would have thought that, in this situation, Donald or Henrietta would have 'phoned a doctor. They did not.

Sketch of the sitting-room

They 'phoned the police, and soon two policemen arrived with an ambulance. They took the evidence of John Donald Merrett and Mrs. Henrietta Sutherland. Donald told them that his mother had been worried about money, and there on the table were the two letters from the Clydesdale Bank referring to Mrs. Merrett's account. Mrs. Merrett was carried to the ambulance to be taken to the Edinburgh Royal Infirmary.

The police action at this point, and later, is quite remarkable. The two officers seem to have accepted at once the idea that Mrs. Merrett had attempted to commit suicide. The two letters from the bank were obviously the reason. They did not search the room, otherwise they would have found a spent cartridge lying under one of the walls. There was the bloody pistol lying on top of the bureau and one of them wrapped it up in paper and put it in his pocket. Knowing from television how suspected objects are treated by the police, you may imagine that this was to preserve whatever finger-prints might be on it. Not in this case. The pistol was wrapped in paper because the officer did not want to get blood on his coat. In fact, nothing whatever was done about fingerprints. Possibly the police did not think it was necessary because Henrietta Sutherland had told them that she had seen Mrs. Merrett fall off her chair and a pistol falling out of her hand.

There is another reason why Edinburgh police officers accepted the attempted suicide explanation so readily. Buckingham Terrace was in a high class district and they would not expect that a murder attempt could possibly take place there. Attempted suicide was the obvious answer, and Mrs. Merrett was put to bed in Ward Three of the Edinburgh Royal Infirmary. This was the ward reserved for people who had tried to commit suicide, and that was a crime. The ward had barred windows and the doors were always kept locked.

On the following day, when his mother was safely in hospital, Donald Merrett went to the Dunedin Palais de Danse and booked out Betty Christie for the whole day. He took her on his motor-bike to the Hawes Inn at Queensferry with its Robert Louis Stevenson connections, where, during afternoon tea, he told her that his mother had shot herself. As far as we know, he did not explain why she should have attempted suicide. Donald and Betty went back to Edinburgh, but the son could not bring himself to spend the night at 31 Buckingham Terrace. He asked his other dancing friend, George Scott, to book a room for him near the Caledonian Picture House, because he was taking Betty Christie there in the evening. Scott arranged a room for Donald in a hotel next door to the cinema.

In her prison room in the Royal Infirmary Mrs. Merrett had made what appeared to be a good recovery. She was quite lucid when talking to the doctor and the two nurses who were looking after her, but she seemed to have no idea of what had happened to her. She told them that she had been sitting at her table writing a letter and her son Donald had been standing beside her ready to post it for her. "Then a bang went off in my head like a pistol," she said.

"Was there not a pistol there?" asked the nurse.

"No," said Mrs. Merrett. "Was there?"

To the doctor she said, "I was sitting down writing letters and my son Donald was standing beside me. I said, 'Go away, Donald, and don't annoy me.'" Then, she said, she heard a bang and remembered nothing more. The doctor revealed the course of this conversation to the police, but they were not interested. They were still convinced that Mrs. Merrett had tried to commit suicide.

Bertha Merrett's sisters rallied round, which was more than Donald did. He visited his mother in the Infirmary only twice, on each occasion taking Betty Christie with him, but she remained in a corridor outside the Suicide Ward while he had his brief interviews. One of Mrs. Merrett's sisters, a Mrs. Penn, who had arrived from the South of England with her husband, persuaded Donald to leave his hotel and return to 31 Buckingham Terrace. The Penns occupied Mrs. Merrett's bedroom and Donald went back to his own room. Apparently he didn't use his rope after that because there was no need to.

Mr. Penn was very deaf but he was not blind. He was in the sitting room one day when he saw a spent cartridge on the carpet just at the foot of one of the walls. He took this cartridge to the police, but once again they were not interested. Mrs. Penn visited her sister every day and one day Mrs. Merrett suddenly said to her, "Did Donald not do it? He is such a naughty boy."

Donald, meanwhile, came up with one of the most bizarre ideas in this bizarre case. He announced to the Penns that he was going to London to consult an eminent detective to see what his verdict would be on the case of Mrs. Merrett. He succeeded in getting money from Mrs. Penn and immediately left for London. His journey from Edinburgh was in a taxi driven by a taxi-driver friend of his. They were accompanied by two girls, one of them under the consenting age of sixteen.

What happened in London we do not know. However, a week later, Donald returned to Buckingham Terrace in an exceedingly bedraggled state. His story was that he and his driver friend had spent all their money on a fruitless visit, because the famous detective apparently couldn't help them. They had, said Donald, to walk all the way back from London to Edinburgh. He didn't explain what had happened to the taxi.

Bertha Merrett died in Ward Three of the Edinburgh Royal Infirmary on 1 April. You may be glad to know that John Donald Merrett actually went to the funeral without Betty Christie. The case of the "suicide" of Mrs. Merrett seemed closed. The Edinburgh police were taking no further interest in it. They seemed to be quite glad that such an unsavoury incident as the suicide of a respectable lady in a respectable area of Edinburgh was now over and no unfortunate details of middle-class life had to be revealed.

The "suicide's" son celebrated the occasion by going on a yachting holiday based at Tighnabruaich. Whether or not he knew of the case of Alfred John Monson we do not know. Thereafter Donald went back to England and lived with various relatives. Eight months had passed and the fate of his mother seemed to have been forgotten.

But the Clydesdale Bank in Edinburgh had not forgotten. They had been investigating the queer business of Mrs. Merrett's cheques and they had got in touch with the

Edinburgh police who reopened the whole Merrett case. The result was that, one day at the end of 1926, when Donald was living with friends in High Wycombe, two Edinburgh police officers arrived and arrested him on the charge of the murder of his mother and 29 Clydesdale Bank cheque forgeries amounting to a total of £457 – a large sum in 1926. The officers escorted him back to Edinburgh, where he was held in custody.

2

"A big romping boy"

Murder trials are not always as exciting as the general public think they are. There's not much room now for trial reports in the newspapers, and still less on television, so it's only natural that what you read or see is a selective affair and it's mainly the high spots of the trial which are the subject of selection. Not only that, but a reader or a viewer should never make his mind up on any such trial on the basis of the information which is conveyed to him by the media.

This, I hasten to say, is not the fault of the media. First, they cannot possibly have the facilities to cover a complete trial (though they did their best in Victorian days, when newsprint was cheap and there was neither radio nor television). The last time I recollect a really big coverage was the trial of the Lanarkshire mass murderer, Peter Manuel. And this brings up another point. By law the media may not describe how an accused person looks in the dock or the witness-box. Thus, if you are sitting in the court, you may see the accused turn pale and speculate as to the reason why, but you may not report it.

Nor can the media represent the accused's accent. In the case of Manuel, the accused spoke with a very strong West of Scotland accent (some called it a "Glaswegian" one), but his words were reported approximately in English. He dismissed his learned counsel and defended himself and, reading the newspapers, some people came to the conclusion that he was a very clever man indeed. If you had heard Manuel speak in court, you might not have thought so.

The fact is that, no matter how remarkable the murder and its circumstances, there are long, boring pieces of evidence – maybe important evidence, but none the less boring to the outside witness. Perhaps this is not true of every murder trial, but it has been true of most of the many trials I have attended as a reporter, or observer.

The week's trial of John Donald Merrett for murder and forgery had its high spots, but it was mainly boring. Nobody seemed more bored than the accused himself. Donald was now nineteen, but looked much older. He had a highly coloured complexion and wore horn-rimmed spectacles. He was six feet tall and built like an all-in wrestler. He had elected not to give evidence on his own behalf, so perhaps he had nothing to look forward to. He spent the week slouched in the dock and even the appearance of Betty Christie in the witness-box did not appear to arouse him.

The trial opened in the High Court of Justiciary in Edinburgh on 1 February 1927. The judge was the Lord Justice-Clerk, Lord Alness. The Lord Advocate, the Right Hon. William Watson, appeared for the Crown assisted by Lord Kinross. The defence was conducted by the renowned Craigie Aitchison KC, with McGregor Mitchell KC, and J. L. M. Clyde, advocate.

This was a fine array of Scottish legal talent so why did the trial have so many longueurs? I have already had something to say about "expert" evidence in murder trials. Usually it is confined to medical "experts", but the Merrett trial abounded in not only medical men, but handwriting experts, arms experts, financial experts and forgery experts. As we have seen, experts are inclined to contradict each other, depending on whether they are appearing for the pros-

Merrett at the time of his trial

ecution or the defence, but always in the nicest possible way. After all, they might be appearing on the other side at some future trial.

Craigie Aitchison did his best to enliven the proceedings. He questioned Mrs. Henrietta Sutherland keenly about her change of evidence. You may recall that originally she said that she was in the kitchen when she heard a shot and then Donald came through and told her that his mother had shot herself. Later she told the police and her doctor that she had gone into the sitting room and had seen Mrs. Merrett falling from her chair with the pistol in her hand. Now she had returned to her original story and explained, in cross-examination, that she had been so excited by the affair that she had said she saw Mrs. Merrett falling from the chair. In calmer recollection, she realised this was not the case.

It seems to me that Rita, who was friendly enough with the accused to call him by his Christian name – not a usual form of address by a servant to a superior at that time in Edinburgh – was taking a suggestion which Donald had put to her to add verisimilitude to an otherwise bald and unconvincing narrative. (W. S. Gilbert always had the right phrase.) Then, when it came to the actual trial, she thought she had better tell the truth.

Although she was given a rather rough time by Craigie Aitchison, she could not be moved from what she obviously knew to be the truth. Nevertheless, the defence succeeded in raising some doubts in the minds of the jury. Women were now allowed to do jury service and out of the fifteen jurors, five were women. It has been said that women judge women harder than men do. That's as may be. But you will see when the verdict on John Donald Merrett is analysed what part the women jurors took in the decision.

If Henrietta Sutherland had a rough time, it was nothing to the roasting which Craigie Aitchison gave Mrs. Penn. For some reason of his own, he had decided to treat Mrs. Merrett's inoffensive sister as a hostile witness. The suggestion at the back of this gambit was that, if Mrs. Penn could influence the verdict against Donald, he would be hanged and the fortune that should be coming to him from his grandfather would be diverted to Mrs. Penn's own son.

Looking at the case from this point in time it would seem that Craigie Aitchison's suspicions were unworthy. Not only did Mrs. Penn simply tell the truth as she knew it about her conversations with Mrs. Merrett, but she did not try to incriminate Donald in any way. Indeed, she seemed to regard it as her duty as his mother's sister to protect him and, if need be, look after him. In any case, no matter how the defence counsel led her up the garden path, she refused to stray. She remained unshaken to the end of her cross examination.

The Edinburgh police made a sorry appearance. They would know, of course, of the Crown's annoyance at the fact that the case had been bungled and that the Lord Advocate and his assistants were left with trying to produce evidence about events which had lain fallow for many months. They could have been happier, of course, if they had had the opportunity to cross-examine John Donald Merrett in the witness-box. But Donald, as I have said, elected not to give evidence, and it was understood that, in murder cases, the Crown would not direct the attention of the jury to the fact that the accused refused to say anything. It's interesting to speculate on what might have happened if Donald had taken his stand as a witness. Here, after all, was the only person who was on the spot when Mrs. Merrett was shot. But the Crown nobly kept to the legal understanding and it was not pointed out to the jury that the accused had refused to give evidence.

Betty Christie had been brought from Glasgow to appear in the witness-box. She had shaken the dust of the Dunedin from her dancing shoes and moved to the other side of Scotland, where she was appearing in the Locarno Club in Sauchiehall Street in her role as dance instructress and bookable partner. She could not really add much to the jury's knowledge because she knew only what Donald had told her. But she could give evidence as to the sort of chap that Donald was. So, when Craigie Aitchison asked her if she would describe John Donald Merrett as just "a big romping boy", she enthusiastically replied in the affirmative.

The forgery side of the trial took up a great deal of time. The Clydesdale Bank had discovered that Mrs. Merrett's bank book had been missing after she had died. And they also discovered that it had been found in the basement of the Dunedin Palais de Danse. Craigie Aitchison pointed out, in his address to the jury, that, if the accused had wanted to get rid of his mother's bank book and took it to the Dunedin basement, he would surely have used the opportunity to throw it into the fiery furnace which provided heat for the Palais.

The bankers and the handwriting experts were solid men. Nobody could fault what the bankers said, and the forgery men were convincing too. They had analysed Mrs. Merrett's handwriting and Donald's as well. They pointed out that nobody signs his or her signature in exactly the same way, but there were the cheques with the same precise signature on each of them. They could also see the marks of the tracings which Donald had made and inked over.

All Craigie Aitchison could do about that was complain, again in his address to the jury, that it was a rather underhand trick of the Crown to include the forgery charge along with the charge of murder.

The two arms experts disagreed politely with each other about the possible use of the pistol and its effects when fired from different angles. There was little to choose between them.

Then came the battle of the giants – the part of the trial that most people were waiting for. The two top forensic medicine men in Britain were alleged to be in conflict. For the Crown there appeared the aging but distinguished figure of Professor John Glaister, whose book on forensic medicine was regarded then as the last word on the subject. (Don't, by the way, confuse him with his son, also Professor John Glaister and a forensic expert, whose most outstanding case was the Buck Ruxton murders at Lancaster.) When High Courts were sitting, you could depend upon it that Professor Glaister Senior would be appearing. In his old age he was apt to be rather short with people, particularly young counsel. I remember one such, in the Glasgow High Court, asking Professor Glaister in the witness box what his age was. The Professor replied, "One day older than it was when I answered the same question in this court yesterday."

His opponent, it must be said, was even more famous than

Professor Glaister. He was none other than the great Sir Bernard Spilsbury, whose opinions seemed to have the weight of law. Of course, he appeared extensively in the London courts so that he had received even more publicity than Professor Glaister had done. Sir Bernard was a noble, impressive figure in the witness box. He, it might be said, boxed carefully for the defence, because he well knew what a doughty opponent he might have if Professor Glaister got his dander up.

As it turned out, the battle of the giants was no more than a gentlemanly fencing match. Glaister did go so far as to say, "The case is barely possible consistent with suicide," but conceded that suicide might be considered a correct opinion by some other people. For the defence Sir Bernard was all for suicide as the reason for Mrs. Merrett's death, and there were the usual arguments about lines of fire, the blackening of wounds, and the handling of weapons. It appeared that women who committed suicide with a pistol did the job quite differently from men, owing mainly to being different in human form. But in cross-examination Sir Bernard agreed that an outside shot was also just possible.

The Lord Advocate addressed the jury in what some observers felt were fairly moderate terms. He had been hampered, of course, by the lack of any real evidence from the police. He put up, as far as he could, a convincing case for the Crown.

For the defence Craigie Aitchison was not hampered (though he might have been if the accused had given evidence) and he gave the kind of address to the jury that was expected of him by connoisseurs of murder trials. Later I saw him often as a most distinguished judge, but I sometimes got the feeling that, as he looked at the defence counsel in some of the cases he heard, he could have been reflecting on how much better he could have done the job.

The last words of his address to the jury on this occasion

Lord Alness

was an appeal for John Donald Merrett. He said, "Send him out from this court room this afternoon a free man with a clean bill and, so far as I can judge, he will never dishonour your verdict."

Lord Alness summed up. The jury retired and, in the course of time, returned. The foreman announced that, on the murder charge, they found the accused Not Proven, by a majority. On the forgery charge they found him Guilty and the verdict was unanimous. Lord Alness appeared to agree that the Not Proven verdict was a suitable one and, as far as the forgery charge was concerned, he decided, in view of the youth of the accused, that he should go to prison for twelve months.

Later William Roughead, who occasionally took a rather misogynous view of life, pointed out that the jury, on the murder charge, had voted five for Guilty and ten for Not Proven, and that the five women on the jury had voted Not Proven.

So John Donald Merrett disappeared from the scene for a spell. But he was to come back in a big way.

3

Love and marriage

In prison Donald didn't do so badly. Perhaps it would be too much to say that he actually enjoyed himself, but he found the life quite tolerable and he learned a lot. Though what he learned did not seem to contribute much to his future life as a reformed citizen. But he did make some important contacts and, though he had not yet attained his majority, he grew ever wiser in the ways of crime.

His relatives on his mother's side, despite any doubts they may have had, accepted the idea that he was not guilty of murder. He was visited in prison, when it was convenient, by Mr. and Mrs. Penn and other acquaintances who gave him the assurance that he had done nothing worse than commit the comparatively small peccadillo of trifling with Mrs. Merrett's bank account. Any hard-up son in his position might have done the same.

One of his most frequent visitors was Mrs. Mary Bonnar, an old friend of Mrs. Merrett. She brought small gifts to the prison and made it clear that she, and everyone she knew, believed implicitly in Donald's innocence. His time in durance vile was lightened by Mrs. Bonnar's stories of her new romance. She was, she said, being courted by a Baron, no less. He called himself Sir William Menzies and had a castle in Scotland. The time came when the romance was consummated and Mrs. Bonnar told Donald, with due middle-aged coyness, that he must now call her Lady Menzies.

Little is known of Baron (or Sir William) Menzies, except for a wedding photograph showing him in full Highland regalia, as befits a Scottish chieftain. It has been suggested by English investigators of the Merrett case that the Baron was an impostor, but this is not necessarily so. True, his name did not appear in Debrett, but in Scotland there are a number of castle estates which carry with them the honorary title of Baron. No less a person than Nicholas Fairbairn MP is the Baron of Fordell because he lives in Fordell Castle. A friend of mine is the Baroness Kilbride, though she prefers to be called Madame Stuart Stevenson. And out at the pleasant little village of Fintry, just over the Campsie Hills from Glasgow, lives Hercules Robinson, the Baron of Culcreuch because he inherited Culcreuch Castle. It is believed that Mrs. Bonnar's second husband lived in the central belt of Scotland. Stirlingshire has been suggested but I have been unable to pinpoint where. The story at the time was that it was a somewhat dilapidated castle, so it may well be a roofless ruin by this time. Mrs. Bonnar was uninterested in castle life (or maybe she had seen it!). All she was interested in was the title and she was known for the rest of her life as Lady Menzies.

Mrs. Bonnar was a staunch Roman Catholic and did not believe that a marriage was valid unless it was conducted under the aegis of her Church. Nevertheless, such is the influence of a title, she agreed to a Protestant marriage with Sir William Menzies. Some time later, when she demanded of her husband that they should also be married in the Roman Catholic faith, he refused. Lady Menzies left him there and then, with her teenage daughter Vera, who had been taught to have the same religious principles as her mother.

This may seem a slight divergence from our tale. On the contrary, it is most important because it had a great effect on

Wedding photo. Baron and Lady Menzies.

the later life of John Donald Merrett. We should never underestimate the influence of religion.

At that time in prison, Donald, I don't suppose, had any other motive in life than to preserve the person of John Donald Merrett. But, when he was released from prison in October 1927, Lady Menzies invited him to join her in her home at Hastings, where she lived with her beautiful daughter. Donald accepted the kind invitation, went to Hastings and was instantly enamoured. Vera, it must be said, was enamoured too. She was just seventeen at the time.

With Lady Menzies and Vera, Donald was quite ready to talk about his time in prison, but he hated to be reminded of his mother's death. He was being supported by the Public Trustee because, when he attained his majority, he would be the recipient of a large legacy from his grandfather – the father of Mrs. Bertha Merrett. Naturally, with some money coming in, Donald made no attempt to find a job of any kind. He spent most of the money which the Public Trustee gave him on a new sports car. This impressed Vera greatly and, two weeks after they had first met, Donald made the pleasant suggestion that Vera should come in his new car for a long weekend.

She agreed at once and off they set, leaving a note for Lady Menzies to acquaint her of their plans – without, of course, telling her of their actual itinerary. Lady Menzies seemed not averse, though she may well have had words with Vera in private. The long weekend soon became known and caused a local scandal in Hastings. It required all of the authority of Lady Menzies to put it down.

The scandal seemed to elate Donald. He and Vera indulged in what was a whirlwind courtship. The wind of love blew so strong that, when Donald suggested to Vera that they should elope to Scotland in his new sports car and get married there, she agreed to the elopement with one proviso. She was a true daughter of Lady Menzies and insisted that any civil marriage should be followed by a ceremony in a Roman Catholic church.

Donald agreed with her at once. He assured her that all would be well. What he did not mention was that, not for the first time, he was in financial trouble. His new sports car was taken back by the firm who had provided it, owing to the fact that he had not met their financial requirements. However, he was not dismayed. He had a cheque book and he was accustomed to dealing with cheques. He bought a second-hand car with a cheque. Other cheques provided a tent and a large amount of provisions and he drove off from Hastings with Vera and her two pet spaniels, which she insisted on taking with her. Perhaps it was the honeymoon influence but she didn't seem to notice that Donald was driving a different car from the sleek sports model.

This time it was too much for Lady Menzies and she organised a posse in Hastings to pursue the lovers and the spaniels. The difficulty for the posse, however, was that, though Donald was assumed to be heading north, they had no idea of what route he would take. Nor did they know that he had changed cars. They were looking for the sports car.

Donald suspected that they would be pursued, but he knew all would go well because he was a firm believer in horoscopes, astrology and What the Stars Foretell. The stars had indicated that all would be well. And so he motored gaily on, scattering dud cheques as if they were confetti. He was a reckless driver and long ago he had left the posse behind.

He chose side roads because they had to find a place where they would be allowed to pitch their tent. Occasionally they spent the night in small hotels, but they had a hotel problem with the spaniels. When, in course of time, they reached Glasgow, Donald visited the Registrar's office in the district of Govan, well outside the city centre, and arranged for them to be married. On the appointed day of the wedding ceremony Donald had to press two passers-by to be their witnesses. Since it was a non-Catholic ceremony Vera didn't count it as a real marriage and kept nagging him, in a nice way, to have their real wedding.

They motored on up into the Highlands and eventually chose a small town with a convenient Roman Catholic church and a consenting priest. After a suitable period of residence, they were wed. On this occasion John Donald Merrett gave his name as Ronald John Chesney, the name he was to use for the rest of his life, although at suitable intervals he affected other names. Whatever name he chose appeared to make no difference to Vera. She always called him Don, though, for convenience sake, I shall now call him Chesney.

They toured Scotland in their tent without any apparent difficulty. Chesney had still his supply of cheques and they were always accepted, perhaps because he was such a big, breezy character and spoke with an English (in other words, a well-off) accent.

But, although Chesney had beaten the Hastings posse, he had not realised that the police in the North of England had been alerted to his cheque-dropping habit and were watching for him. Chesney, Vera and the two spaniels had got as far south as Newcastle and decided to spend the night there. They pitched their tent in a field on the outskirts of the town and had hardly got their billy-can on the boil when the police suddenly appeared. They took Chesney to the New-castle police headquarters, where he was charged with steal-ing by forging cheques. The police, accepting his name as Chesney, did not realise that as Merrett he had already served a year's sentence in Scotland for the same offence, but they kept him in custody.

The police also advised Vera to return to her home at Hastings. Lady Menzies was contacted and so the new Mrs. Chesney and her faithful hounds went back to a rather mixed reception. Her situation was not made any happier by the message from Newcastle that her husband had been sentenced to six months' imprisonment. Lady Menzies made it clear that she disapproved of the elopement and the wedding, but even more of the outrage to her dignity as an aristocrat. However, she softened as she gleaned some details from her daughter of the inheritance which was coming to her new son-in-law when he reached the age of 21.

By the time that he was released from Newcastle jail, she was ready to overlook Donald's little peccadilloes and take him back to her bosom. So Chesney returned to Hastings and for a year or so kept, as they say, a low profile. It took him some time to be accepted again in Hastings, and there were people who wondered why he had changed his name.

But there came the glorious day of 17 August 1929, his twenty-first birthday. He received word from the Public Trustee that his grandfather had left him £50,000. All criticism of his past life was cancelled and the cries of "For he's a jolly good fellow" grew as the champagne circulated. From then onwards champagne was Chesney's favourite drink – although he liked whisky, brandy, gin, rum and various other beverages as well. If he was flamboyant at the age of eighteen it was nothing compared with his attitude on attaining his majority.

He bought a big house in Hastings and lived like a lord. Lady Menzies was in her element. He had a tennis court, went in for horse riding, turned part of the house into a ballroom with bar trimmings (perhaps he wanted to cherish the memory of Betty and the Dunedin Palais de Danse), he played rugby football, went to boxing matches, and, when he required additional female companionship, visited Soho.

Apart from throwing his money about, Chesney did one thoughtful deed. He settled the sum of £8400 on his wife. Vera was to receive the interest for her lifetime. If she died, the £8400 would revert to Chesney.

After a while life in Hastings seemed to pall on Chesney. Maybe he felt it was too far away from Soho. He uprooted the family and flitted. He bought a shop or two, but they seemed to fail. He also bought a small yacht and took up sailing in earnest. This, like his thoughtful settlement on Vera, was to prove particularly valuable in his later life. The most important transaction which Ronald John Chesney made at this time, however, was to buy a mansion at Weybridge. It had twenty rooms and almost the first thing he did was to turn one into a bar and another into a gambling room.

The Chesneys adopted two children, a boy and a girl. They had none of their own. Chesney installed a staff of six and gave wild parties (at least, they were considered wild in Weybridge) every weekend. He gave up trying to run normal business affairs, and spent more and more time in sailing his yacht. Someone in the yachting world told him one night of the advantages of going into smuggling. Chesney thought it over. Big profits, no income tax. He decided to try it out on a small scale. Right away he found this was the life. He enjoyed the excitement and he enjoyed the money. He grew a beard and wore an ear-ring when such pieces of costume jewellery were unheard of as far as men were concerned.

Soon he found that what he must do was to get into the big time. The trouble with Chesney was that he always needed money, especially for his drink bill and his gambling. One of his Soho contacts tipped him off that there was a successful crew of smugglers in the East End of London and that they were always ready to try out a new recruit.

It did not take Chesney long to join the smugglers in London. After all, he could prove that he had already been successful in the business, even if only in a comparatively small way. The East End boys owned a well-doing brothel in the Mile End area and they also used it as their store for smuggled goods. They operated from Southend and had never been caught.

Chesney soon got into their good books. He had examined the operations closely and suggested that he should buy a

Ronald John Chesney in Malta just before the War

private aeroplane, which he would use mainly for smuggling reconnaissance. His fellow smugglers agreed enthusiastically. Chesney soon learned to pilot a two-seater 'plane and was able to provide valuable information to Mile End headquarters.

But, while flying had its own excitement, he yearned for more adventurous activities. He always wanted to be in the thick of the action and reconnaissance flights were hardly that. And so he sold his private 'plane and also his mansion at Weybridge and bought an old Bristol Channel pilot cutter, which was so spacious that it had not only room for the contraband but for the Chesney family as well.

Towards the end of 1935 he set sail in the *Gladys May* for the Mediterranean, taking the whole family, including Lady Menzies, with him. As far as they were concerned, this was a wonderful holiday in the sun, instead of staying in wintry

Vera Chesney at the beginning of the War

England. There is nothing to indicate that either Vera or Lady Menzies knew that they were on a smuggling expedition, although it was about that time that Vera started to drink heavily. Chesney had a big party in every port and the gin flowed free. He had an engaging habit, as far as his lady guests were concerned, of offering them some water with their gin, in the Navy style. What they didn't know was that the jugs which contained the "water" were half full of gin.

Chesney's special smuggling runs were from North Africa and Italy to Spain. His cargoes were usually arms and drugs. The arms run was especially profitable. He was paid £1 for every rifle he landed in Spain, and between that and what he made on the drugs, he was quite happy to get a profit of

£1000 on each of his trips. It worked on the return voyage too, for he smuggled cigarettes, liquor, gold and diamonds from Tangier to Italy. No wonder he announced when one of his parties was going really well that his favourite character was Barbarossa.

Rows with Vera grew more and more frequent. She could see the point of a champagne or gin party because she was assisting in the celebrations, but she could not stand Chesney's gambling. And she was right because the time came when her husband was so much in debt all round the Mediterranean that the only thing to do was up anchor and sail for home.

Back in London they got a mortgage on a fair-sized house in Ealing. Vera had discussed the situation with her mother and they had the idea of turning the place into a guest house for old people who either had money or had relations who were glad to pay to keep them out of the way.

From the point of view of the two women this venture was modestly successful. Vera, although her drink problem was still with her, was able to run the house with the aid of her mother and a small daily staff, and Lady Menzies was in her element playing lady bountiful to the guests and being constantly addressed by her title.

Ronald John Chesney was not so happy. He had lost his life of adventure and, though he tried to make up for it by associating with criminal elements in the East End, he could not recapture his first fine careless rapture. He took part in various "jobs", but they were on rather a small scale for a man who liked to do things in a big style.

He did develop artistically, however. He was taught by experts how to forge a passport, an essential for any travelling man. He became highly accomplished in faking passports and might have made a career out of it. But then, in the autumn of 1939, Lord Beaverbrook started announcing, "There will be no war this year or next year either." That was the signal to Chesney. He knew that if Beaverbrook said anything, the opposite would happen. Sure enough, World War II broke out. It may have been patriotism, it may have been profit, or it may just have been the surge of adrenalin which came to him when he thought about his days at sea. Whatever it was, Ronald John Chesney joined the Royal Navy on 3 January 1940.

4

War and peace?

It seems strange, looking back in time, that a man with Ronald John Chesney's criminal record would be welcomed into the Royal Navy and given an almost immediate commission. But, as those of us who served in the Armed Forces in the Second World War know, some very strange things happened in the early days. Chesney, of course, had certain qualifications which would appeal to Naval recruiters. He was tall, outgoing to say the least, energetic and, as apparently a man among men, a first-class recruit. Add to that his sailing experiences all over the Mediterranean – many a man who applied to join the Navy during the war had hardly any knowledge of the sea at all. Some had got no farther than a holiday cruise or two.

At any rate, beard, ear-ring and all, Chesney was welcomed into the Navy. Here was adventure at last and a wonderful opportunity to get away from the guest house for geriatrics, the dull life in London, and the responsibilities he was always trying to dodge. It also meant getting away from his wife, although she had responded immediately to his gallant gesture in joining the Navy and they were friends again. Perhaps she was not averse to seeing Don out of her way.

Chesney was a great success in the Navy. His dashing style appealed to his officers and in less than three months he was

Chesney after promotion to lieutenant

promoted to the rank of lieutenant. He was now given temporary command of various small ships of war. So impetuous was his entry into harbours, quays and ports that he was soon nicknamed "Crasher" Chesney. He was the life and soul of the Ward Room.

In 1941 "Crasher" was given command of a motor gunboat. He was sent out to the Mediterranean, his happy hunting ground for so long, now the scene of a confrontation between the British and Allied forces and a German Army led by the famous Rommel. When the British redoubt at Tobruk

Chesney commanded this motor gunboat in 1941

was threatened, Chesney's command was changed to a schooner. His job was to ferry supplies across the Mediterranean to the beleaguered garrison.

This job had Chesney in his element. He was famous, especially among the Tobruk troops, as the captain who brought his schooner in to land, wearing a top hat instead of the regulation headgear. Ashore he was always accompanied by his bull terrier and they were familiar figures in the big camp at Tobruk.

It did not take long for Chesney to realise that he could take up his old job of smuggling, even if there was a war on. It would have been dangerous, of course, to smuggle out of Tobruk any of the supplies he was taking in, though occasionally he managed to remove stocks of cigarettes, coffee and sugar. But the one thing the defenders of Tobruk were not going to miss was the big number of Axis vehicles which had been abandoned in the desert. So he worked on a very profitable sideline, shipping Axis cars and what spare parts that could be found from Tobruk to Alexandria.

Chesney's smuggling came to an end when Rommel attacked Tobruk in force and the order came in that Allied troops were to be evacuated. Instead of taking out cars from Tobruk, he was ferrying out soldiers to the ships brought in for the evacuation. He loaded a new batch of men on his schooner and was starting out into the Mediterranean when his ship was hit. Shells were flying all around him. Another vessel came in to help and the soldiers were all able to board her.

But Chesney saw that his ship was sinking. He refused to be rescued and plunged into the water with his bull terrier and swam ashore. The Germans were so near that a Nazi patrol was coming down the beach as Chesney reached it. They had seen what was happening and burst out laughing, pointing out to sea. Chesney turned round and saw that his schooner had not sunk at all. It was already being towed out by the rescue vessel. He turned round to his captors and started laughing too.

He was taken to a compound for prisoners, but he soon saw that conditions were chaotic. The German troops were far too busy to be bothered about their prisoners at that moment. Where could a prisoner go in any case? When Chesney saw his opportunity he simply walked out of the compound and no one stopped him. He had trudged several miles through sand when Italian troops, who were backing up the Germans, saw him and recaptured him.

Chesney landed up in Modena Prison, where the Italians were in command and life for a POW was not too bad. Indeed, his only real worry was when he went into the prison library to get something to read and found the William

Roughead book on his trial in Edinburgh on the shelves. Although he was now wearing a beard and was considerably older, he was recognised by some of his fellow prisoners who asked him if he was John Donald Merrett. Chesney denied it completely. But soon afterwards the book of the Merrett trial disappeared from the library shelves and was never seen again.

The daring buccaneer found life in Modena Prison tedious. He pretended to be ill and was sent to the prison hospital. There he acted so convincingly that the Italian doctors decided he should be repatriated. He was exchanged for two Italian officers who were in a military hospital somewhere in Britain.

When he came home, stories of his exploits had preceded him and he was considered a local war hero. The Navy cast an approving eye over him too. After a suitable period of rest and rehabilitation he went back to the Navy and was promoted to the rank of lieutenant-commander. He was sent to a shore job at Kirkwall in Orkney, an important if remote Naval station not far from the great anchorage of Scapa Flow. He was able to take his wife with him and, what with hero worship and pleasant enough living compared with conditions in the South, Vera seemed to fall in love with her husband all over again.

After a year in the Orkneys, Chesney was posted to another shore job, this time in Germany. The war was over in Europe and the Allies were trying to bring some order to a defeated and demoralised country. Wives were not welcomed in Chesney's new job and, in any case, Vera felt it was time she was returning to help her mother, who had been running the guest house on her own. She returned to London and her husband settled down to his new job of trying to put things right in Germany.

Chesney's methods of helping were somewhat unusual. He discovered right away that the opportunities of "liberating" German goods and valuables were immense. You just went into any unprotected building, be it factory or mansion house, and helped yourself to what was there. There was also the black market. Germans were short of food, cigarettes and soap, to say nothing of myriad other objects and goods. Chesney smuggled in these commodities and bartered them for the Germans' gold, cameras, antiques, carpets and almost anything that took his fancy.

German women also took his fancy. He started womanising again – something he had found rather difficult in the Orkneys! But Vera was back in Ealing and facing the realities of post-war London. She wrote long letters of complaint and kept asking her husband to send her money. He wrote back and said that, on his lieutenant-commander's pay, he couldn't. At this time he was making an estimated £500 a week on his smuggling and black market transactions. But he had his reputation as a party-giver to keep up and he was also spending a lot of money on women.

There were plenty of attractive women about Buxtehude. One of them was a German girl who had succeeded in escaping from the Russian Zone of Germany. She had managed to get a temporary job in Allied headquarters in the town. Her name was Gerda Schaller and she was very beautiful. Chesney fell in love with her at first sight and took her to see his quarters. Gerda couldn't believe her eyes and said later that she now knew what Aladdin's Cave looked like. The rooms were crammed with fine furniture, carpets, curtains, objets d'arts and there were cupboards stuffed with jewellery, cameras and ornaments of all kinds. Below in a cellar there were crates of champagne and all the German wines.

Soon the time came when his rooms were overflowing and Chesney had to take a house in Buxtehude as a spare store. By this time Gerda and he were living together. Life seemed perfect for Chesney if it were not for the begging

Lt.-Commander Chesney at Buxtehude

Gerda Schaller

letters from his difficult wife. He went home on leave and there was an almost continuous succession of rows with Vera. It was worse than usual, he found, because he kept thinking of what he was missing in Buxtehude. He gave Vera some money, but he had been spending so much in Germany, particularly on parties and gambling, that he was in danger of becoming hard up – in his terms, at any rate.

When he got back to Buxtehude he decided to celebrate by taking Gerda Schaller on a trip to Paris. He had his eye on a big car which was said to have belonged to a high ranking Nazi officer. When the time was ripe, he took the car, picked up Gerda and drove South to France. They arrived in Paris without mishap, but what Chesney did not know was that the Military Police were on his trail. In Paris he had no sooner sold the car and prepared to spend the money than he was arrested on a charge of stealing it. This was a Royal Navy Court Martial case, of course, and he spent six weeks in custody before he was tried. Gerda had to appear as a witness, but was not held in custody. At the Court Martial he made the plea that it had all been a bit of a prank and a way of making the Nazis look foolish. But he had sold the car and the sentence of the Court was four months' imprisonment.

Gerda Schaller went back to Germany, but this time she elected to live in Hamburg rather than return to Buxtehude. So, when Chesney was released, he decided to return to his wife in Ealing. Vera had become an alcoholic and the rows were more frequent. Lady Menzies did her best to calm things down, for she still thought of her son-in-law as slightly misled but adventurous and a great character. After a while Chesney could stand no more of life in London. He had kept in touch with Gerda and, as soon as he could escape from Vera, he went to Hamburg.

Chesney took up smuggling once again. He liked Gerda to be with him so he forged a passport for her so that they could travel on jobs all over Europe. He was drinking as hard as

Police file pictures of Chesney at the time of his imprisonment in France

ever. On one occasion he was delivering a load of coffee and aspirins to a contact in Belgium when he crashed his car. He escaped with only trifling injuries and saw that the car was such a write-off that the coffee and aspirins were in mounds across the roadway. There was only one thing to do. He set fire to the wreck of his car.

From Hamburg he was now writing to Vera pleading for a divorce, making it quite clear that he was living with Gerda Schaller. As a well brought up Roman Catholic, Vera would not countenance divorce.

He travelled widely on his smuggling activities and not always with Gerda. Paris seemed unlucky for him. He was caught there on a smuggling charge and it's significant that he appeared in court under the name of John Merrett. Obviously his past was now known to the police. His sentence was four months' imprisonment, but he appealed and it was reduced to two months. He had hardly served his sentence when he was employed by an international gang to carry forged banknotes to Switzerland.

By this time Ronald John Chesney was well known to the international police, especially as he was now travelling everywhere with the readily recognised Gerda Schaller. They were arrested on suspicion in France and the police detected that Gerda's passport was forged. When they appeared in court, Gerda was sentenced to six months' imprisonment for using a forged passport, and Chesney to four months for forging it.

He did not wait for her release. He thought he would be safer in England and went back once again to Vera in Ealing. She had never stopped writing to him for money, so in May 1949 he went back to local smuggling and gave some of the proceeds to her. His luck failed him once again. He was caught smuggling nylons and sentenced to three months' imprisonment.

When he was released, in January 1950, he decided to dish Vera, as was his wont, and returned to Germany. He knew that Gerda Schaller had gone to live in Cologne, and searched for her there. They lived together for a few weeks but Gerda could not forgive him for deserting her in France, and left him. He was caught with a car full of drugs at Newhaven and once again went to prison – this time for a year.

In prison he had time to think over his misfortunes and his lack of money. Then he remembered, perhaps not for the first time, the settlement of £8400 he had made on his wife. Vera was to enjoy the interest during her lifetime but, if she died before Chesney, the £8400 would revert to him. The solution for his troubles was obvious – Vera would have to die. Out of prison, he made his criminal contacts once again. He went around some of his more violent friends offering a "contract" worth £1000 for the death of his wife. Much to his surprise, not a single contact would accept his contract.

Back to Germany he went and met an amenable German girl whom he installed in Gerda's place. Three months went by and Chesney felt that smuggling was not enough; he had to get that £8400. He left his new German girl friend and returned to Ealing, where there was a sort of reconciliation. He spent most of his time in London making his contacts once again, but without any joy. There was only one thing to be done. He would have to kill his wife without help.

One day, in El Vino's bar in Fleet Street, he was pondering over the solution when he noticed a man at another table who looked familiar to him. Yet he didn't know him. All of a sudden it came to him. Except for a slight difference in height the man opposite was his double – at least, he was the double of the Chesney who had been clean shaven. Here was the solution at last. Chesney made careful enquiries and found that his double was a newspaper photographer named Chown. He had very little trouble in getting a picture of Chown and with it he went back to Germany and forged a new passport – for himself.

This passport contained Chown's picture, his name and address and all other necessary details. To make sure he was right, Chesney shaved off his beard, looked in the mirror, compared the reflection with the passport and decided it was just what he wanted. He had given up wearing his ear-ring when he left the Navy, so he didn't need to do anything about that.

He wrote to Vera telling her that his fortunes had taken an upward turn and that he would be able to give her all the money she wanted. He said he would be back in Ealing soon and life would be just as it was in the good old days. Then he bought a paperback in English entitled *The Brides in the Bath*. It dealt with a celebrated murder case in England in which a gentleman married one wealthy woman after another and, by some amazing coincidence, each was found drowned in her bath.

When he judged the time was ripe, Chesney left Cologne airport as Chown, flew to London, and read *The Brides in the*

Bath on the way. In London he bought two bottles of gin and carried them to the meeting with Vera in Ealing. He had 'phoned her from the airport and told her not to mention to anyone in the guest house of his visit. And so husband and wife met and fell in each other's arms. Vera was already rather drunk and she was delighted that she would soon have all the money she wanted. Her Don kept filling her glass, latterly with neat gin. In the course of time she passed out completely.

Chesney went into Vera's bathroom and filled a bath. Then he went back and checked that Vera was completely unconscious. He lifted her, carried her through to the bathroom and put her, fully clothed, into the bath. He held her under the water until he could tell that she was drowned. With all the gin around, his theory was that it would seem that Vera had drunk herself into such a condition that she had run herself a bath and had fallen into it.

He wiped the gin bottles clean of fingerprints and made certain that there was nothing in the flat to incriminate him. Only Vera had seen him come in to the guest house and now he had to make sure that no one would see him go out. He looked down the stairs to the hall and there was not a soul to be seen. He had timed everything so that the guests would all be at dinner when the moment of escape arrived. So he went silently down the stairs.

Chesney had just reached the lobby when the kitchen door opened and Lady Menzies appeared, holding a tray with a steaming coffee pot on it. She must have expressed surprise at Donald being there. Donald knew that, if she lived, she would identify him. He seized the coffee pot and used it as a weapon on her head. She fell to the floor but he kept on hitting her until he was sure she was dead. There wasn't a sound from the guests, who were two rooms away. Chesney rose from his crouch over the body, disappeared from the guest house and took a taxi to the airport.

Police investigations at the Ealing guest house

He flew back to Cologne and spent the next day or two composing a letter to his solicitors saying that he had heard of the unfortunate death of his wife and reminding them that he would now be entitled to claim £8400 from his wife's estate.

Chesney got a dusty answer from his solicitors, who indicated that there was considerable interest on the part of the police concerning the deaths of his wife and his mother-in-law and that the police intended to visit him shortly in Cologne. He telephoned one or two of his London contacts and they told him forcibly that they didn't want to have anything to do with him.

Three days later Ronald John Chesney, alias John Donald Merrett, took his revolver, went to a wood on the outskirts of Cologne and shot himself. The body was identified by the police and also by Gerda Schaller. When it came to Chesney's funeral in a Cologne cemetery, the coffin was placed on a low trolley and pulled to the grave by a cemetery worker. It bore one wreath and was followed by only one person – Gerda Schaller. Doubtless Chesney would have had satisfaction in knowing that the picture of his last journey was published in papers all over Europe.

A doctor friend of mine who lives in Edinburgh served in the Royal Navy during the Second World War and had quite a deal to do with lieutenant-commander Ronald John Chesney. "He was always the life and soul of the party," he told me.

Last journey

That may be so, but he was certainly the death and despair of other parties.

As far as John Donald Merrett is concerned, one wonders what would have happened to him if he had been found Guilty in the High Court of Edinburgh of murdering his mother. He would, of course, have been sentenced to be hanged, but it seems likely that, taking into account his youth and the doubts about how Mrs. Merrett died, he would have been reprieved and sentenced to life imprisonment. In that case, he could have been released from prison when he was in his early thirties, and he would immediately have inherited £50,000. And the Second World War would be raging. I leave it to you.

VERDICTS ON THE VERDICT

William Roughead described the verdict Not Proven as "that indefensible and invidious finding". One Scottish judge described it as a verdict which cast a slur, and was intended to cast a slur, on the panel (the man or woman in the dock). I have mentioned already that Madeleine Smith was most indignant that she was found Not Proven of murdering Pierre Emile L'Angelier. And I must say that, in my own experience of murder trials, going back for 55 years, I have seen persons leaving the court free when it was as certain as anything could be in this uncertain world that they had committed the deed.

One of the best books I have read on the subject, *Not Proven* by John Gray Wilson (Secker and Warburg, 1960), has this to say: "Probably the great majority of the legal profession in Scotland approve of the Not Proven verdict. But they do so in silence. Those who speak or write of it tend to be critical, even strongly so: publicly expressed admiration comes from outside."

Well, Sir Walter Scott, who had plenty of experience of the law, referred in his diary to "that bastard verdict, Not Proven. I hate the Caledonian *medium quid*." And in 1906 Lord Moncrieff, a distinguished Scottish judge, called the Not Proven verdict "both theoretically and historically indefensible".

On the other hand, Judge Gerald Sparrow, in more recent times, wrote of Scotland's three verdicts to England's two, "I have often thought that the distinction typifies the different spirit of Scottish and English Law; the Scottish being the more logical, the English more sporting."

It has been argued that, if Scotland's three verdicts are to be reduced to two, the one to be discarded is Not Guilty. This makes sense to me – though I have had no training in the law. On the Continent an accused person has to prove his or her innocence of the charge, In this country the Crown has to prove that the case for Guilty is proven. So surely the verdict is Proven or Not Proven.

If I may be permitted to give the Lion Rampant a wee wave, may I say that I hope the upholders of Scots Law do not give up the verdict of Not Proven. We have lost too many Scottish things already.